MW00718435

THE DAY THE WALLS
CRIED

To Monique
Thanks for your
support!
Shawn.

ALSO BY SNOOK

KARMA'S KISS
THE DOWN TURN
ISSUES OF THE HEART

COMING SOON
KARMA'S KISS 2

THE DAY THE WALLS
CRIED

S N O O K

 AMARQUIS PUBLICATIONS

Amarquis Publications, LLC
P.O. Box 34224
North Chesterfield, VA 23234

Library of Congress Control Number: 2014949609

ISBN-13: 978-0-692-28534-3
First Amarquis Publications Paperback Edition September 2014

Printed in the United States
Cover art & interior designed by Indie Designz

THIS BOOK IS DEDICATED TO FAMILIES
LIVING WITH DISABILITIES.

ACKNOWLEDGEMENTS

I thank God for seeing me through another project that's dear to my heart. Each word represents a lesson. I can only hope that the message is received. This book is dedicated to families living with disabilities. It may be a parent, son, daughter, sibling, aunt, uncle, or cousin. These families must be strong to endure the many challenges others know nothing about. I know something about it.

I would like to thank all of my readers that support each one of my books and events. A special thanks to my family and friends for your continued support. I'm not one to name names and give special shout outs, because I don't want to leave anyone out. I love and appreciate each and every one of you.

Much love,

Snook

PROLOGUE

On a hot August day, a beautiful, bouncing baby boy was born to forty year old Jasmine Peterson. She'd found herself in the Medical College of Virginia's maternity ward. It was filled with screaming women in the midst of labor. There were mothers ranging in ages from young teenagers, to women in their mid-forties, giving birth on that hot, humid Saturday. Doctors and nurses raced up and down the hallways as babies were born into the world, one after the other.

Jasmine was single and lived with her mother. Her pregnancy wasn't planned. She had a few serious relationships, but none resulted in pregnancy. Therefore, she was under the assumption that she couldn't get pregnant. She was unaware of her pregnancy until the sixth month, when there was no way of denying that the bulge in her belly was life.

Before the baby was taken to the nursery, Jasmine counted all of his fingers and toes. She snapped her fingers on each side of him, to see if there was a response to the sound. However, the baby didn't respond. He continued to cry out as he did moments after he was delivered. She wrapped him in the receiving blanket and handed him to the waiting nurse. She pointed to her ears and then pointed at the baby.

"Yes, we will check his hearing," the nurse responded.

Jasmine looked over at her mother, shook her head, and snapped her fingers twice in her own ears.

"That boy is just fine, Jasmine. The way he is sounding off, he has a set of lungs on him. He can hear. I know he can," Jasmine's mother, Ruth, responded.

Jasmine shook her head "no" more aggressively.

"He's going to be fine. You remember all the times I read to him and talked to him? Didn't he respond to me? He would kick and move all around your belly when he heard Granny's voice. I prayed for him and I know he can hear and talk. You just watch and see," she said.

"Jasmine, you just relax and let the doctors take care of him. He looks just fine. You did an awesome job," Pearl said. Pearl was Ruth's younger sister, there for the miracle birth of the baby. She handed Jasmine a cup of water to drink that the nurse sat out for her.

"I can't believe she was in denial all of this time. It took almost six months for her to realize that she was really pregnant and wasn't getting fat," Pearl said.

"I told you she was pregnant," Ruth said.

"I told her she was pregnant and she would just shake her head. I know she didn't just think she was only gaining weight in her midsection, did she?" Pearl asked, as she laughed.

Jasmine read their lips and knew exactly what they were saying. She smacked her lips, rolled her eyes, and turned her back on them. They did not respond to her display of dismay. They were used to it.

"Did she decide on a name for him yet?" Pearl asked.

"King Solomon Peterson, after my dear husband. Rest his soul. If he's anything like his grandfather, he will live up to that name," Ruth said.

"He shall be called King. That is a real good name for him. He can carry on the name, since you and King never had a son," Pearl said, as she winked at Ruth.

Ruth looked at Pearl and rolled her eyes. "She is so worried that he is going to be like her. I told her that he was going to be fine, because he is a blessing. I prayed and prayed that he wouldn't be like her, but if he is, we will deal with it."

"I know she's worried. She doesn't want the boy to go through life not hearing a thing or being able to talk. Her life is different from ours. We can't relate to being deaf or not being able to express ourselves with words. As much as *you* like to run your mouth, you would go crazy, Ruth."

"However God sees fit. We made it through with her, and we will make it through with him."

They sat in the hospital room with Jasmine as they waited for the baby boy to be returned. Jasmine was quiet. She wore a despondent look on her face.

About an hour later, another nurse appeared, wheeling the baby into the room.

"Here is baby Peterson, Mommy," the nurse said. She wheeled the baby slowly in the hospital bassinet towards Jasmine's bed. She immediately cheered up when she saw her baby boy. With her mother's help, she sat up slowly to hold her baby.

As the nurse situated items in the bassinet, she gave instructions to Jasmine with her back turned towards her. "Here are the diapers and wipes in this drawer," she said, pulling out a drawer on the bassinet, revealing neatly stacked small diapers and wipes. "If you have a hard time breastfeeding, I've placed bottles here." She pointed to the bottom of the bassinet, where two bottles were placed. "And, here are some extra t-shirts and blankets."

As Jasmine waited and watched the nurse shift around, she clapped her hands in frustration to get the nurse's attention. When the nurse finally looked up, she reached for her son.

"Oh, okay," the nurse said nervously. She looked at Ruth, who stood beside Jasmine's bed.

"I'm sorry, but she has to read your lips to know what you are saying. She's deaf," Ruth said.

"Oh, I didn't know. I'm sorry. I actually know sign language," the nurse said. She immediately began to repeat herself through sign language to Jasmine and in return, Jasmine responded with sign language.

The nurse handed King to his mother and left the room.

"I told you about clapping your hands at people. That is so rude," Ruth said.

She saw what her mother said, but ignored her.

Jasmine was in heaven with her baby boy. She kissed him and kissed him until there were no other places to lay any more kisses. She continued to mouth, "I love you" to her baby, as he gazed into her eyes. Jasmine held him close to her bosom. When he began to whine, she placed him at her breast. As if he'd been nursing for days, King took to his mother. Ruth stood over them and watched the mother and son bond. She looked back at Pearl, who was also caught in the moment.

Ruth rubbed Jasmine's arm to get her attention. "This is the time that you should mold his head," Ruth said.

4

Ruth gently removed King's yellow cap from his head, revealing a head full of straight, dark hair atop of a cone-shaped head. While he nursed, she admired him.

"I've never seen that girl smile so much. This is just what she needs," Pearl said.

Ruth nodded in agreement.

Softly starting at the crown of his head, she rubbed down the front, sides, and back of his head, smoothing down his straight, dark hair that curled at her touch. She was sure not to press too hard on his soft spot, where the skull was yet to fuse. Jasmine watched attentively. Ruth pointed to the soft spot. Pointing out her pointer and middle finger on each hand, she placed her right hand over her left hand and hit them together twice, saying, "Careful."

Jasmine placed a fist to the side of her head, moved it away slightly, and extended her pointer finger to say, "I understand."

Ruth nodded and placed Jasmine's free hand gently on King's head. She did as her mother showed her, while she nursed her baby boy.

"My babies," Ruth said.

Ruth walked over to join Pearl on the other side of the room, giving Jasmine time alone with the baby.

"Speaking of babies, do you know who his father is?" Pearl leaned in to ask.

"You just mind your own business. Do you see him here?" Ruth replied.

"I was just asking. Is it that tall fellow that is always coming around with flowers and those nasty boxes of chocolates?"

"No. He isn't the father of this baby," Ruth said.

Jasmine looked at them. She placed her hand over her mouth, so that Jasmine couldn't read her lips.

"He didn't spend more than five minutes around us, before she would run his butt away. We know who the father is, but he doesn't want to be involved in this, so I told him that we didn't need him."

"Humph! Deadbeat!"

Ruth took care of both her daughter and grandchild, but still allowed Jasmine to be a mother. She was there to assist in teaching Jasmine and King how to communicate with each other. She knew some sign language, enough to effectively communicate with Jasmine.

CHAPTER 1

King was an only child and grandchild. He was spoiled and had just about everything he wanted. As he grew into a toddler, his favorite spot was in front of the television where he watched cartoons.

They lived in a house with a lawn and big backyard, and all was well, until his grandmother fell sick. The trouble was with her heart; she couldn't walk a few feet without getting tired. King noticed how his grandmother began to slow down. She needed his assistance at times, during which he was glad to help. His mother had to take care of her until she died; that was when life changed. After his grandmother's death, they had to move out of their home and into the projects.

Tossed into a world different than his own, King had to grow up fast. In a fast-paced environment, he had to learn how to survive. Children were forced to grow up faster than they needed to. Never would his mother have known that moving to the projects would change both of their lives forever.

King and his mother moved to the most dangerous housing project in the city of Richmond. They couldn't afford to stay and maintain the rental property where they lived with his grandmother. His mother, being deaf, received a social security check, along with public assistance and food stamps each month. Not having a job and her only having a small source of income made public housing their only option.

There, King saw his first, and sadly, not his last dead body. The first dead body he'd seen was a man, shot to death, lying in the middle of the street. The man was walking from the store when he was shot and robbed. An opened bag of white powdered donuts lay above the dead man's head that was covered in blood. That sight sent King running home to vomit. From that day forward, the sight of powdered donuts made his stomach retch.

Waking up to the coldness of concrete walls was something to get used to. Their old house was warm, comfortable, and full of love. His grandmother took excellent care of him and looked out for both him and his mother. He never had to worry about his mother. He was now the man of the house, and had the responsibility of protecting his mother as she protected him.

His mother was a strong woman and a fighter. She protected King tooth and nail when needed. Everyone in the neighborhood knew that she wasn't to be messed with. She put in work, never letting anyone take her disability for a weakness, although they tried. There was a time when King was being jumped only a week after moving into their new apartment. His mother came outside with a butcher knife, threatening all the kids and the mother that refereed the fight. No one got stabbed that day, but she kicked ass up and down the sidewalk.

King's earliest memory was of his grandmother always cooking and cleaning. There were times when she would sit and enjoy her stories on television, but she always worked.

King's grandfather died before he was born. Even though he never met him, he felt close to him. His grandmother spoke of him every day that he could remember. She would say, "If your grandfather was alive, he would do this or that."

Every day, she dusted off his photographs and talked to him. At first, he thought she was crazy for talking to a picture of a dead man, but he then realized that was her way of keeping him alive. His presence could be felt in their home, because she refused to let him be forgotten.

Jasmine was a beautiful, loving woman. Her touch was soft, and she always made everything better. Growing up with a mother that was different from everyone else was difficult for him to understand. He didn't understand why his mother had to be the one that was unable to speak or hear, while all of his friend's mothers and family members could. He felt alone in a sense that he was the only one with a mother with such a disability. She couldn't hear his cries or joys. There was so much he wanted to tell her and talk to her about. Knowing she was unable to connect in that manner, he would shut down most times and hold it all in. He wished she was like everyone else. King felt he was different and alone with no one to relate to him.

It wasn't until he met the son and daughter of his mother's friend, Patricia, when they went over for a visit that King was able to see he wasn't alone. His mother wasn't the only one, and there were other children that could relate to him. That relieved him of the feeling of loneliness, which allowed him to be more certain of himself and his situation.

CHAPTER 2

After school, King, and his friends walked home in the brisk winter weather. They lived two blocks from their school, in a housing project called K.C. Court, a.k.a. Kill City. A murder or violent crime happened there at least once a week. Most families scrambled to pay their bills and feed their children there. The children tried to act as if they weren't poor. Hiding food stamp books while paying for food at the corner store was the norm. Most of them received free lunch at school and lived with little friends called roaches. There were the regular drunks pacing the streets, begging for change, and the dope boys that worked the block.

"Your crackhead momma," King said.

"Your ashy foot momma!" Eric shouted.

"Your momma so ugly, your daddy left and never came back. That's why you don't have a daddy," King said.

"Chill before somebody get mad. You know he always wants to fight if you say something he doesn't like," Richie said.

SNOOK

Richie was King's best friend and next door neighbor. Richie lived with his mother and little sister. They became friends quickly and immediately clicked. They had many things in common; they both loved sports and collecting sports trading cards.

"Shut up, Rich! You don't have nothing to do with it. If they want to get it in, let them. Don't get me started on those dirty ass shoestrings. Look like you been jumping in mud or something," Mike said, pointing down at Richie's sneakers.

"Fuck you! Tell your momma to get you a haircut. I'm sure she make enough money on her knees to pay for a haircut. When was the last time your head was touched by clippers? You're walking around here with lint balls in your hair. Pick that shit out," Richie said.

"You always want to talk about somebody momma!" Mike said, embarrassed by Richie's brash response.

"Your momma so dumb, she can't hear or talk," Eric called out to King as they walked.

They waited in anticipation for a fight to break out. Like any other day, they cracked jokes while they walked home. As always, things had the potential of getting serious, especially with the "momma" jokes. It started out in good fun, but quickly went sour as Eric and King went in on each other.

It was freezing outside, and King's nose dripped with snot. It was the last day of school for winter vacation. He wasn't scared to fight Eric, but he wasn't sure if it would be one-on-one. Eric had three brothers and two sisters. If one fought, they all fought, and their mom might, too. They were on their block, and everybody was outside. He was trembling from cold winds that whipped through his thin winter coat.

12

"Oh, no he didn't say that about your momma! King, I know you're not going to let him talk about your momma like that. That's just dirty," Shamere, Mike's sister, said. She was on the heavy side and was teased unmercifully.

"Shut up, big momma!" Eric said angrily.

Shamere rolled her eyes and sucked her teeth. She continued to walk with the group, but slowed to walk behind them.

"You gon' let him talk about your momma like that?" Richie asked, daring him to back down from a fight.

"Don't be talking about my momma. Say it again and see if I don't whoop your ass," King said, staring him in his eyes.

Eric was tall, light skin with freckles and curly red hair. His face was either red from anger or the freezing winds. The group stopped walking as King and Eric faced off. The group of children that walked behind them caught up to see if a fight would happen. They all began to chant, "Say it"! and "Hit him"!

"Your momma so dumb, she can't even—" Eric tried to finish his sentence. Spit from his mouth flew in King's face.

King pulled back his fist and punched Eric in his mouth, before he could get the rest of the words out. He tackled Eric, knocking him to the ground, and King pounded on Eric's face with his fist. Eric tried to fight King off as he swung wildly with one hand, and blocked hits with the other. He was so heated by his anger, he didn't even feel the cold or hear the chanting around him anymore. He punched him in his face, until Eric's older brother, Kirk, kicked him off him. Kirk kicked him in his kidneys; King grabbed his side and fell over onto the ground. The sharp pain wrapped around his left kidney and stayed there. He couldn't breathe for a moment.

"Get off of him before I beat your little ass!" Kirk yelled, towering over him. The crowd stopped chanting and Kirk stepped away from him.

It took a few seconds for King to realize that the chanting suddenly stopped. King was confused. He didn't know why everything became so quiet all of a sudden. He looked around to see what everyone was looking at. It was his mother. She was petite and no taller than the group of children. She walked towards them with a look that could kill. She motioned for King to get up. He picked himself up from the freezing ground and dusted his clothes off. His nose ran even more, so he wiped it with his coat sleeve. He walked over to her and she led him to their apartment.

No words were exchanged between the two, but he understood. If she could speak, she would tell him how proud she was of him for standing up for himself and that she would never let anything happen to him. She pointed upstairs after she helped him out of his coat. He headed upstairs to wash his face and hands. When he came back downstairs, he found his mother sitting in the living room.

King went to the kitchen for his after school snack, cereal. He opened the fridge and there wasn't much inside. It was close to the end of the month, and food always ran low around that time. He reached for the carton of milk, opened it, and smelled it to be sure it wasn't spoiled.

A bowl and spoon waited on the table. He sat and poured a bowl of cereal. A few roaches fell into the bowl, along with the cereal. King watched in dismay as the roaches scattered around the bowl. Disgusted, he began to kill the roaches that fell out onto the table. He ran the bowl and box of cereal over to the trash can. He took a mental note to be sure to put a rubber band on the bag inside of the box to keep the roaches out. Instead of having a bowl of cereal, he put on a pot of hot water for Ramen noodles.

In the living room, his mother went through his book bag, pulling out the stack of papers that he failed to show her. He could tell by the look of disappointment on her face that she wasn't pleased with the grades. He failed his last two math tests. She felt his presence and she shook her head at him. He put his head down in shame. The last thing he wanted to do was disappoint his mother. There was also a letter requesting a conference with his mother.

After she had gone through all of the papers, she turned towards him, still shaking her head in disappointment. She pointed at the math tests she held in her hand, demanding an explanation.

"It's hard. I'll try to do better next time," he said. He shrugged his shoulders. There was no doubt in his mind that he could do better. He was still adjusting.

They were on their own. There was no one to look after them and he was scared. He was forced to be the man and protect his mother, sooner than he was ready to. He knew that people would try to point out his mother's disability as a weakness for them both and he wasn't going to let it happen. Being that she was deaf, he had to be her ears and mouth.

She smiled and reached for him. At twelve, King was taller than his mother. He already stood five foot five and had a slender build, with a medium brown complexion. King walked over and sat down on the sofa next to her.

15

She placed the papers in his hand and gave him a very serious look. He knew that meant that she didn't want to see those grades again.

His mother kissed him and pointed upstairs. He knew she loved him. Even though he'd never heard her say it, she showed her love. Her doting smiles said, "I love you". In every hug and kiss, he felt her love.

He stomped up the stairs, because he knew she wouldn't let him go outside and play with his friends. He was careful not to stomp too hard, because she would feel it. He knew Richie would knock on the door to play football sooner or later.

He went to his mother's room to watch television. Noticing that his mother finally placed his grandmother's picture on her dresser, he walked over to see it more closely. The picture of his grandmother in her housedress and black-rimmed glasses, holding him in a baby blue sleeper, put a smile on his face. He had all good memories of his grandmother and loved her deeply. To know that she loved him gave him a sense of peace and certainty that she still looked over them.

CHAPTER 3

Dreaming that he was falling off of a cliff, King fought to wake himself from the nightmare he had. He tried to turn over, but it felt as if he was held down by something. The wind whistled passed him as he quickly descended to his demise. A rocking motion interrupted the fall in midair. Confused, he was awakened by a shaking bed. His mother stood over him with the most beautiful smile. Her smile could light up a dark room.

"What?" he asked. He yawned and wiped the hard crust that formed in the corners of his eyes.

His mother tried to tell him that it was time for him to get up, but all that came out was a high-pitched sound as she tried to mouth words. She'd only taught him basic or common sense sign language. To say "hamburger", she would pat an imaginary beef patty between her hands. To ask if he was ready to eat, she would spoon imaginary food to her mouth. To tell him to bathe, she would pretend to wash by scrubbing an arm. Despite the communication barrier, they understood each other as if they had a language of their own.

Their project apartment felt cold and empty. There wasn't nearly as much furniture or pictures on the walls as the old house. There were really no reminders of his grandmother or the old house. They did keep the sofa and floor model television, however. Other than that, they didn't have much at all. His mother did the best she could with what they had.

King rolled out of the bed and threw on a pair of jeans, sweatshirt, boots, hat, and coat, and then headed outside. As he pulled on one of his gloves, his thumb went through a hole. Yanking off the gloves, he noticed that there was another small hole in the palm of his other glove. He grabbed two pairs of clean socks from his drawer instead. He pulled on the white tube socks over his hands.

It had snowed the night before, and he couldn't wait to have a snowball fight with his friends. He looked outside to see who was outside already. Alonzo, Mike, and Richie were already outside, playing football in the snow. He assumed they'd already knocked on the door for him and his mother didn't feel it.

On his way out the door, his mother pointed at the decorated Christmas tree. She was proud of the tree from the huge smile on her face. They'd had the same tree at his grandmother's house every year. The artificial Christmas tree sat in a corner of the living room, closer to the front window. The same green and red bulbs, lights, nutcrackers, reindeers, and fake icicles adorned the tree. She'd even sprayed a can of white snow on it. He smiled at her to show his appreciation and headed out the door. King opened the front door and a stinging cold rushed into the house. He hurried and closed it behind him.

"Man, come on. We been waiting on you for a minute,"

Alonzo said. He threw the football hard at King's chest and he caught it, eyeing him angrily.

Alonzo and King didn't really like each other. They cracked on each other and gave each other a hard time every time they were around each other. Alonzo was Richie's cousin and that was the only reason they played together.

"I'm here now. Let's go. Me and Richie against y'all," King called out. He glared at Alonzo, who he knew would oppose, but this time, he didn't.

"All right. Then, we going to the corner store. I have ten dollars in food stamps that I stole from my mama," Mike said, waving a single food coupon in the air.

"Let's go now. I'm hungry," Richie said. He rubbed his stomach.

"Let's play a quick game so I can dust him," King said. He whispered to Mike, "When he get the ball, I'm going to knock him on his ass."

They played a quick game in the snow. They laughed more than they played as each one of them slid and fell in the snow. After the game, they walked to the corner store, wet from the melting snow on their clothes. King shivered every time his wet jeans brushed against his skin. His jeans became stiff. He wanted his share of the ten dollars, so he had to endure the pain of the cold.

"Hey. Don't think I forgot about that shit yesterday. Watch your back," Kirk said. He stood in front of the store, with a Mad Dog 20/20 he'd slipped into a brown paper bag.

"What's up, son?" Tone said, bumping fists with only King. "Yo, leave him alone. Stop fucking with them little boys. Worry about them clowns across town trying to rob your broke ass," Tone said to Kirk, in his Northern accent. Tone was twenty years old. He was older than the group of boys he hung out with. He always wore his hair in two, straight to the back cornrows that hung to the middle of his back. His family was from New York and moved to Virginia when Tone found himself in trouble.

"Yeah, you better be glad your daddy here to save your ass," Kirk said sarcastically. He spat in King's direction, missing his feet by inches.

"Go ahead, son. Nobody's going to fuck with you. Not even his punk ass," Tone said. Tone shoved Kirk, but Kirk didn't do anything. He kept sipping on his bottle.

King looked at Kirk with a cocky smirk as he and his friends walked past. He wondered why Tone always jumped to his defense and called him "son" all the time. He assumed that was what most New Yorkers called people.

King kept his eyes in front of him and ignored the comment. There was no way he was going to get his ass beat in the snow. If he did have to fight, he knew Richie and Mike would have his back, but it was just too damn cold for all that.

"Get what y'all want, just make sure it don't cost more than two dollars," Mike reminded them as they entered the store.

They split up and headed in different directions in the store. The store owner always kept a close eye on them every time they came into the store. King didn't know about the rest of them, but he would get more than his two dollars' worth. Cold drinks were in the back, so he headed to the cooler to get a Yoo-hoo. Walking down the candy aisle, he watched the owner watch him. A young woman approached the counter with an arm full of items. She carelessly dropped everything on the counter, dropping a bag of chips on the floor.

Kneeling down, King picked up candy from the bottom shelves. He managed to slip a Suzy-Q that he picked up when he first entered the store into his coat pocket with his right hand. King browsed the candy aisle, acting as if he was trying to decide what he wanted. Richie joined him on the aisle with an orange soda, potato chips, and sunflower seeds. He eyed King suspiciously.

"What are you getting?" Richie asked.

"This and some candy," King said. He held up the Yoo-Hoo. "I want a pickle if they have some more."

Richie gave him a knowing look, but he didn't say anything. They exchanged sly grins as King confirmed that he had much more than he showed.

"Come on, man. I'm ready to pay for this shit," Mike called out from the counter. Alonzo, Richie, and King headed to the counter, dropping their items on the counter. Mike handed the owner the food stamp with a cocky smile.

"Where is the book?" the owner asked. He peered down from behind the counter.

"What book?" Mike asked angrily.

"The book you tore this food stamp from. Every time you come in here, I tell you the same thing. Are you taking them from your mother?" the owner asked, peering down on Mike.

"Hell no! That's the way she gave it to me. If you don't want it, then I can take it to the other store. They don't complain like you do," Mike said. He turned to walk away while the rest of us stood there, hoping that the owner would change his mind.

"This is the last time you come in here with these loose stamps. Do you understand me?" the owner asked.

Mike walked back to the counter with a big smile on

21

his face. He knew exactly what he was doing. The owner rung up the items and handed Mike back his change. They gathered the bags and left. Outside of the store, they separated their items.

"He always complaining, but he take those loose food stamps anyway," Mike said, before he gulped down a 7UP.

"I'm cold as hell. I'm going home," Alonzo said, turning the corner towards his house. "I'll be back out later on."

All the boys were freezing, so they went home. King's mom was in the kitchen cooking breakfast. She prepared corned beef hash, sausage links, eggs, and toast. He went upstairs to change into dry clothes and joined her at the table. They sat in silence eating their food; she watched him eat and he watched her. King finished his food and joined her in the living room to watch television. She put her arms around him as she always did and he melted into her arms. He wished that they could talk to each other, because there was so much he wanted to say. He wanted to tell her about his day and how excited he was for Christmas.

CHAPTER 4

It was Christmas morning. King could hardly sleep the night before and had only slept a few hours. He ran into his mother's room where she was sound asleep.

"Ma! It's Christmas!" he yelled. He jumped up and down on the bed, waking her. She rolled over and looked at him as if he had lost his mind. She slowly rose from her bed and followed him downstairs.

There were many gifts under the tree but his eyes landed on two large, neatly wrapped gifts. He hoped it was what he wanted as he ripped off the wrapping paper. It was an electric football game he'd asked for two years before, and she was finally able to get it for him. He ripped open the second largest gift with a white envelope attached, and there it was; an Atari game system. He gave his mother a hug and kiss and thanked her. He knew she had to make a sacrifice to purchase that gift for him. She pointed at the small individually wrapped gift. King told everybody that he would get an Atari for Christmas; although, he knew it was a slim chance of that happening on his mother's small income. He was almost positive that Aunt Pearl helped to make it possible. His mother picked another gift from under the tree and gave it to him to open. The smile on her face warmed the room as she relished in King's joy. He had what he really wanted, but he opened the rest of the gifts, anyway. There was a boom box, trading cards, and a video game for his Atari under the tree. There were also individually wrapped socks, shirt, gloves, underwear, and a new pair of blue jeans. King was thankful for everything.

"Thank you," he said. He hugged and kissed his mother.

His mother's girlfriends came over; Sonya and Patricia were his mother's dearest friends and they were also deaf. They met at a school for the deaf and blind many years ago and remained close friends. Sonya was King's godmother. They both came with a gift, which he appreciated.

King was busy playing his game. He needed to learn to play before he played against anyone else. He knew a few people that had one, but he didn't get enough playtime to master the game. In the kitchen, Sonya and Patricia communicated with his mother through sign language. Their hands moved quickly, often making slapping sounds as they signed. He watched them as they helped prepare Christmas dinner.

It wasn't long before Richie knocked on the door, bragging about all the stuff he got for Christmas.

"Look at my new bike!" Richie said.

"That joint is sweet, but look what I got," King said.

"You want me to come in there? I'm not leaving my bike out here to get stolen. You must be crazy," Richie said.

"Well, hurry up then," King said.

"Man, nobody better not steal my bike," Richie said. He walked his bike closer to the apartment and stood it on its kickstand. He followed King into the house, but stood inside of the door so that he could keep an eye on his bike.

"I have an Atari!" King said.

"Man, how you get one? I wanted one too," Richie said.

"My mama," King said.

"You're lucky. I'm going be over here all the time now," Richie said.

"Hey, y'all coming out or what? I have some new teams for the football game," Mike yelled from outside.

Richie went outside to show Mike his new bike while King went to his room to get his electric football game. Richie rode his bike while King and Mike played electric football. A short while later Alonzo joined them.

"I got next," Alonzo called out, sitting on the stoop. He pulled out a cigarette and lit it. "I'm gon' whoop your ass." He took Mike's place.

"We gon' see about that," King said.

"Your punk ass thinks you better than me. You ain't," Alonzo said.

"I am, bitch," King said. He matched his angry tone.

"Just play. Y'all always beefing," Mike said. He tried to diffuse the situation.

Alonzo and King went into the game with every intention of winning. They exchanged words several times during the game. Alonzo became angrier each time King scored, his brows narrowed and mouth tightened.

"Forget you!" Alonzo jumped up and stepped on the electric football game.

"Man! Forget you!" King said, jumping to his feet.

They fought and King lost the fight. Alonzo was bigger and older, but King gave him one hell of a fight for stepping on his game. After that day, Alonzo and King didn't beef as much, because they both knew where they stood.

CHAPTER 5

King, Richie, and Mike rode their bikes down the Turnpike. King rode on the back of Richie's bike as they headed towards a nearby residential neighborhood. Some of the children they went to school with lived there. Some of the boys were cool, but others looked down on them, because they lived in the projects and the other boys lived in houses. Therefore, in return they stole their bikes for parts and money.

It was a ten-minute bike ride from where they lived. The cool air whipped passed them as they pedaled to their destination. The cold air-dried King's eyes as he rode. He needed to blink and rub them to keep them moist. Mike led them, because he was smaller and faster than the rest of them. Richie was right behind him with King. Richie breathed heavily as he pedaled with King's weight.

"Yo! Let's take this shortcut over here," Mike said.

He turned onto a street that they would normally pass when going to that neighborhood. Their normal turn was two streets away. Richie and King followed behind him.

"You better know where you're going," King shouted out.

"I know where I'm going. I came this way last week when I needed tires for my bike. If we go the other way, they might see us," Mike said.

"This better be a shortcut. It don't seem like it," Richie said.

"Man, shut up. I know what I'm doing," Mike said.

Mike slowed down when they came to an intersecting street. Richie did the same.

"I knew he didn't know where he was going," Richie said.

They came to a complete stop on the side of the road. Mike had a sly look on his face.

"Let's go down this street first and see if we see any bikes. This time, you better move faster and do like I say. Last time you almost got us caught with your scary ass," Mike said.

"I wasn't scared. You saw that dog chasing me. Next time you do it then," King said.

"Come on," Mike said.

They turned right at the intersection that led to a cul-de-sac. They scanned the houses as they rode. They searched the front yards and as far back as they could in the backyards.

"Stop! I see one. On the side of that brick house," King said.

"Where?" Richie asked.

"Right there! It's parked against the house," King said.

King pointed at a red and black bike propped against the side of a house. A long, graveled driveway led from the street, along the side of the house. A car was parked in the driveway.

"That's you right there. Go get it," Mike said.

King stepped off the bike. He looked around them to see if anyone had come outside.

"That's what I'm talking about. Man, hurry up before we leave your ass," Mike said.

King shot off running towards the house and ran past the car in the driveway. His heart pounded as soon as his feet hit the gravel. Sure enough, the gravel made his presence known. The gravel screamed out under his feet and speed. His adrenaline kicked in. As soon as he was on the side of the house, he turned towards the street. Richie and Mike were in their take off stance. Their bikes faced out of the cul-de-sac as they looked back at him. Richie waved his hand to tell him to go ahead.

King hopped on the back of the bike and began to pedal fast. It was hard to ride the bike on the gravel, but as soon as he hit the paved street, he took off. He pedaled so hard that his feet slipped off a few times. Richie and Mike were far ahead of him, but he quickly caught up. They didn't stop until they hit the Turnpike to catch their breath. There wasn't any other way back to their apartments. They ran the risk of getting caught on the busy Turnpike.

They made it back to K.C. without getting caught and one bike richer. When they got back, the police were just arriving. Blue lights and sirens sped past them on the street. The boys didn't hesitate, following the action. They followed the police car to the back of the complex where people were standing around a dumpster near Mike's apartment. The boys rode their bikes as close as they could. Outside stood Mike's mom, Bunny. She cried and was consoled by her mother and a friend.

"No! No!" she screamed out.

Mike dropped his bike and ran over to his crying mother. Richie and Mike watched from where they were.

"What the hell happened? You see anything?" Richie asked.

29

"No, but why are the police looking in the dumpster?" King asked.

"I don't know," Richie responded.

"Yo, Mike," King called out.

Mike jogged back over to where he left King and Richie. His head hung low and his eyes were red.

"What happened?" King asked.

"My mama's boyfriend, Shoota is dead. They killed him and put him in that dumpster," Mike said.

"What? Somebody killed Shoota?" Richie said. "Oh, shit. It's going to be hell to pay for that. I ain't coming out for the next couple days, so don't knock on my door."

"You already know. It's going to be a bloodbath around these parts," Mike said.

"Damn, he was taking care of y'all and everything," King said.

"Yeah man. He was a good dude," Mike said. "I hate to see my mom like this. She's messed up behind this."

"What are y'all gon' do now?" Richie asked.

"I know what I'm gon' do. He told me if anything happens to him, to make sure I took care of a few things for him," Mike said.

Shoota was the man around K.C. that supplied work to anybody that stood on those corners. If he didn't supply it, then it couldn't be sold around K.C. For someone to take out Shoota was a play for his crown. He'd lived with Bunny for five years and when he came into their lives; things changed. Bunny got high and neglected Mike and Shamere. They lived with their grandmother, who had to step up and be their mother. Shoota tried to get her cleaned up, but she still fell off the wagon. He included her children in most of the things that they did and made her pay more attention to them. For that, Mike respected him.

Mike went back with his mother as the boys waited to see Shoota's body removed from the dumpster. It felt like forever before they were finished taking photographs and poking around in the dumpster. Finally, the coroner arrived and shortly after, the body was removed.

With every dead body that he saw, he was more determined not to have his life end in the streets. It was the most demeaning way to die. The realness of the fact that death was all around him hardened him. For Shoota to be killed and disposed of in an overfilled dumpster meant that no one was safe in K.C.

Winter vacation came to an end quicker than any of the boys wanted it to. Over winter vacation, King made a few new friends around the neighborhood and got along well in his new environment. He even had older guys starting to look out for him by giving him money, and making sure no one messed with him, especially Tone.

CHAPTER 6

Back in school, one of King's teachers treated him as if he had some sort of disability. Since his mother was deaf, she just assumed he had a hearing problem. After the teacher would give the class instructions, she would repeat them again, just for him.

"King, do you understand what the assignment is?" Mrs. Fisher asked.

"Yes. I always understand the assignments, Mrs. Fisher," he said.

"I just wanted to make sure that you heard me. Well, carry on." She walked back to her desk.

He could feel all eyes on him and heard some laughter around the room. He was embarrassed for the last time. He had to do something about the constant humiliation.

"Retard," William said under his breath. The class erupted in laughter.

William was the class bully. King watched William torture their classmates, but he wouldn't give him the opportunity to get to him. Every time King saw him coming, he went the other way.

"You don't have to repeat everything for me. I can hear just fine, Mrs. Fisher!" King shouted.

Mrs. Fisher looked up from the papers she was grading. Once she realized that he was the one with the bold tone, she looked at him under her eyeglasses.

"King, did you say something?" she asked.

"Yeah, I said I can hear just fine. Stop repeating everything for me," he said.

"I'm not singling you out. I just want to make sure that my directions are clear at all times. I'm sorry if I made you feel uncomfortable."

He felt that he was under attack. It was bad enough that it was freezing in the classroom and everyone had to wear their coats. Of all days his mother made him wear his big winter coat, the biggest feather filled coat in the closet. Every time he moved, he was stuck by feathers and the floor around his desk started to accumulate those same fallen feathers.

"Retard," William repeated. He coughed the words into his hands.

"Fuck you, fat boy!" King shouted. He wasn't going to let William punk him in front of the entire class. None of King's friends were in his class, so he would have to go at that one alone.

"Fuck you!" William shouted.

"Boys! Stop using foul language in my classroom! William, do not call anyone else out of their names. We are all intelligent individuals," Mrs. Fisher said. She raised her voice, but she never moved from behind her desk.

William was seated two desks behind King and there was no way that Mrs. Fisher could stop him before he reached William, considering she was still glued to her seat. King eased off his coat, flipped over his desk to cause a distraction and ran to William's desk.

William's eyes bulged when he saw King heading for him. King hit him with a three-piece, knocking him from his seat, one to the mouth, one to the nose and one to the jaw. William fell from his seat and King kicked him in the face as hard as he could with his boots. Just as his adrenaline kicked in, Mrs. Fisher grabbed him by the back of his collar and dragged him out of the classroom into the hallway. King didn't put up much of a fight with her.

The entire class laughed at William. Some students were out of their seats standing over him, pointing and laughing in his face. He deserved it, because he bullied most of the class.

"King, what has gotten into you? Why did you hit William?" she asked.

"He called me a retard! You heard him!" King shouted at her.

"That doesn't give you a right to put your hands on him. I'm sorry, but you have to go to the principal's office. William could be hurt and you could be suspended. That is not the way to handle your problems."

"That's what he gets!"

"William, come out here," she called into the classroom.

William came out into the hallway with a bloodied nose and mouth. His lip was twice as big as it was before the fight.

"Yes, Mrs. Fisher?" he asked. He avoided eye contact with King, acting as if he wasn't there.

"Go to the nurse. I will be there in a minute," she said.

He walked slowly down the hall to the nurse, cupping his bloody nose. King smiled and almost laughed as he watched. Mrs. Fisher looked at King out of the corner of her eyes and shook her head. He shrugged his shoulders.

She escorted him to the office. The receptionist greeted Mrs. Fisher, and she and Mrs. Fisher exchanged looks. He knew they were secretly talking about him, but he didn't care.

"Is Mr. Phillips available?" Mrs. Fisher asked the receptionist.

"Yes, you can go on back," she said.

Mrs. Fisher took King by the arm to the principal's office. She knocked softly on the door.

"Come in," Mr. Phillips said loudly.

"Wait here," she said.

She opened the door and went into the office, leaving him standing at the door. The door was left slightly open, and he could hear the two of them whispering. He tried to hear what they said, but couldn't make any sense of it.

"King, come in," she said.

King walked into the principal's office and sat in the chair directly in front of his desk without being told. Mrs. Fisher closed the door behind her when she left. King took a quick look at the office since he'd never been in there.

"Mrs. Fisher tells me that you were just in a fight in her class. Is this true?" he asked.

Mr. Phillips spoke in a tone that commanded his attention and told him not to try and bullshit him. Although, from where he sat, he could tell that he was a big man. His hair was cut low and completely gray. He wore a full beard that was also fully gray. He looked at King expectantly through his glasses.

"I did, but he called me a retard and everybody laughed at me," King said.

"I know that made you mad, but we do not tolerate fighting. If someone does something to you like call you a name or hit you, then you should tell your teacher. Your teacher is capable of handling the issue. Since you decided to handle it on your own, now you are going to have to be punished."

King looked at him, and then back at the clock hanging on the wall behind him. He was hungry and it was almost lunchtime.

"Do you understand?" Mr. Phillips asked.

"Yes," King said. He looked down at the floor.

"We have to call your mother to come and get you. You are going to be suspended for three days. Do you know your phone number?" he asked. He picked up the phone receiver from his desk and placed it to his ear. He looked for him to call out the numbers for him to dial.

"I don't have a phone," King said in shame.

"If you don't give me your number, I can still get it. I am giving you the opportunity to tell me."

His nostrils flared and the wrinkles in his forehead protruded. King shrunk down in his seat.

"We don't have a phone. My mom can't hear," he said.

Mr. Phillips slammed down the phone and sat back in his chair. He swayed side to side in his chair without taking his eyes off King. "What do you mean she can't hear?"

"My mom is deaf. She don't talk either."

He studied him for a few seconds and began to relax his shoulders.

"I see. Well, I'm going to send you home with a letter for your mother. For the remainder of the day, you are to stay in the office," he said. He looked at the silver watch on his arm. "It's about lunchtime, so let's go," he said.

He moved away from his desk and walked around towards King. King followed behind him. They were serving everyone's favorite, barquitos. Barquitos were deep-dish mini pizzas, filled with a taco-flavored meat sauce, topped with cheddar cheese. It was the best meal that Richmond Public Schools served, in King's opinion. He walked into the cafeteria with the principal to get his lunch. Everybody watched as King had to trail behind the principal with his lunch tray. He ate his lunch in the office. King was pissed that he wasn't in the cafeteria with his friends, because he had already paid Ashley three dollars in advance for her barquito.

Mrs. Fisher sent his book bag and classwork to the office. Burying his head in a science book, he pretended to read until it was time to go home. The receptionist handed him a sealed envelope with his mother's name on it. He'd never been suspended before but knew that his mom would be upset. The plan was to explain what happened in an attempt to get her sympathy. He figured she would be proud that he stood up for himself, even if she couldn't tell him.

CHAPTER 7

At the end of the school day, King met up with Richie and Mike outside the school. He zipped up his coat and put on a skullcap to shield from the cold. Richie had to be freezing in his thin green jacket, and he didn't have on a hat. King could see him shivering. It wasn't anything he could do to help his friend.

"Come on, man. It's freezing out here!" Richie yelled.

King wasn't in a hurry to get home. He walked slower than usual. His head hung low as he kicked rocks or anything that he could find in his path.

"He's scared he gon' get his ass whooped by his mama," Mike said.

"Shut the fuck up, Mike. Your ass the main one getting his ass whooped for stealing all the damn time," Richie said.

"If it was me, I would throw that letter down the sewer. Right down there." He pointed to the sewer as they passed. "I always throw letters to my mom right down there," Mike said.

King thought about it for a second and then decided against it. *Where would I go for three days without getting caught?* Instead, he kept walking and thought about how disappointed his mother would feel about his suspension. The disappointment was something he didn't want to see on her face.

They reached Mike's street first and they all gave each other dap. Richie and King continued walking.

"Your mom not gon' do nothing to you. She's one of the nicest moms out here. I ain't never seen her hit you. What are you so scared of? It's not like she could fuss at you or nothing. I'm not trying to be funny or nothing, but you're tripping," Richie said.

"It's not about that. You don't understand," King said.

Richie and King reached their apartments.

King's mother was waiting at the door as she did every day. Richie's mom was at work and he let himself in.

"Hey, I'm going to play sick tomorrow," Richie called out. He stepped out of King's mother's eyesight.

"Cool," King said. He didn't want her to know his plans.

Inside, his mother gave him a hug and a kiss and then held her hand out for his book bag. Sliding each arm slowly out of his straps, he practiced what he would say. Handing over his book bag, containing his science book, notebook, and the envelope addressed to his mother, he then he looked away from her gaze.

King went into the kitchen for an after school snack. There were three brand new boxes of cereal on top of the refrigerator. Before he left for school, there wasn't any. He knew that the refrigerator was loaded. He walked faster to the refrigerator and opened it. He was right; his mother made it to the grocery store.

He reached for the full gallon of milk. His heart

stopped when he heard the tearing of an envelope. Suddenly, he lost his appetite. A high-pitched sound echoed from the living room that he often heard when she wanted him to come to her. He walked back to the living room slowly with his head hung low.

"Sorry," he said. He was sure to mouth the word exactly.

She held the letter up to his face, demanding an explanation.

King began to ramble, stuttering over every other word as he explained what led to the suspension. She couldn't read his lips, because he spoke so fast. She placed her hands on his shoulder and gently pointed to his lips. That meant to slow down so that she could read his lips. He took a deep breath and slowed down. He tried to sign as much of the story as he could. King wasn't fluent in sign language, so he did the best that he could. He could sign that he was sick, hurting, where he was going, what he wanted to eat, and a few other things.

After he had told his side of the story, she laughed a little. She took in a deep breath and shook her finger at him. She wasn't happy about what happened, but she understood. She pointed to the front door and shook her head "no", indicating he was on punishment and couldn't go outside to play.

She cut on the floor model television and he sat on the floor in front of it. Eventually, he fell asleep.

～～～

The smell of fried chicken and the sound of laughter awakened him. He sat up as his bones ached from lying on the hard floor. Wiping his eyes, he walked into the kitchen and found his mother and her friend Sonya. They were in conversation with their hands and they laughed loudly.

Noticing King, Sonya turned around and reached for him. She gave him a hug and kiss. His mother stood over the chicken, frying in the cast iron pan on the stove. Sizzling and popping came from the pan as she placed more chicken down into the hot grease.

His mother turned her lips up and proceeded to tell Sonya about the fight. Sonya gave him a high five and put up her fists as if she was boxing. He laughed at her and so did his mother.

King sat at the table, watching the two of them go back and forth until the chicken was done. His mother fixed his plate first and they ate in silence, only exchanging glances. They had their own way of communicating with each other and they understood each other. There were some frustrating times; however, when King and his mother didn't understand each other.

King ate his dinner, bathed and went to bed. As he lay on the bed, he thought about how he would convince his mother to let him go to Richie's the next day. He wasn't sure if Richie would be able to play sick or not, but he hoped that their plans worked.

The next morning his mother didn't wake him, King's internal alarm clock did. He almost jumped up, but quickly realized he didn't have to go to school. He lay back down and went back to sleep.

He woke up again around ten o'clock and found his mother downstairs. She already cooked and was at the kitchen table eating her breakfast. He was anxious to go next door.

Pulling out a chair beside her, she patted the seat, inviting him to sit next to her. He walked over to her, and she put her arms around him and kissed the top of his head. In her arms, he felt loved and safe. Her love radiated through her touch and closeness. He enjoyed their time together.

"Can I go next door?" King asked, as he pointed towards the apartment next door.

She looked confused and shook her head "no".

"Richie stayed home today."

She looked at him suspiciously.

"Please," he begged.

She hesitantly nodded, "yes".

King leaped from the chair and ran upstairs to brush his teeth and to get dressed. He raced down the stairs and into his mother's waiting arms.

"I love you," he said, kissing her.

She signed, "I love you". King did the same.

King walked next door and knocked hard. He didn't know if Richie would be home or not. After no answer, he knocked again louder. He heard someone running down the stairs. Richie opened the door, smelling of Vicks VapoRub.

"Hey, you're early," Richie said.

"And, you stink," King said, holding his nose. He walked into the apartment.

"It was all part of the plan," he said.

King followed him upstairs to his bedroom. His mother was at work and usually came home shortly after they were out of school.

King sat down at the electric football game that he left on his last visit. They had played for hours before their stomachs reminded them to eat. "I'm hungry. I'm going home. I'll be back," King said.

"Do you hear something?" Richie asked. He fumbled the football.

"Hear what?" King asked.

They stopped playing to listen.

"Did you hear that?" Richie jumped up with fear on his face.

King walked over to the television and turned it down, because he didn't hear anything.

That was when he heard a noise coming through the wall. Richie's bedroom shared a wall with Jasmine's bedroom.

King's heart skipped a few beats. He walked over and put his ear to the cold concrete wall and Richie did the same. They faced each other, both wearing faces of concern. King heard his mother in a struggle, screaming. At times, her voice was muffled and others pierced his ears. He could hear flesh being hit, furniture moving and things falling to the floor. Her screams echoed seeming to shake the walls between them.

Grunts and growls came from an unknown voice. He could hear furniture scraping the floor with each sound of heavy pounding. They looked at each other in horror at the painful screams that came through the walls. The walls cried out. At first, they just stood there in shock, not knowing what to do. When a blood-curdling noise pierced his ears, he wanted to go through the wall to save his mother. Through the walls, he listened to his mother cry out in horrifying agony.

"Call 9-1-1!" King shouted to Richie.

King took off out of the bedroom and down the stairs. He jumped down two steps at a time and then ran next door to his apartment and turned the door knob. It was locked. He knew something was wrong, because his mother always left the front door unlocked for him to get in and out of the house. She would have never locked him out.

King banged and kicked the door so that she could feel it. No one came to the door. He lifted the mail slot to look inside. From what he could see, no one was downstairs. Nothing seemed out of place.

Then he saw someone's feet slowly walking down the stairs, leaving behind bloody footprints, but he couldn't see their face. They walked past the apartment door, calmly heading to the back door.

King ran around the building to catch the person leaving out the back door, but when he reached the back, no one was there. He could hear sirens in the distance, so he knew help was on the way.

He ran back to the front of his apartment, where he saw Richie standing. The police were pulling up.

"I called my mom. She's on the way," he said.

King went back to the front door and banged on it again, calling out to his mother. Richie joined him in beating down the door.

"Mom!" King called out.

The officers approached them. "Which one of you called?" an officer asked.

Richie explained what they heard. King stopped banging, realizing that she couldn't come to the door. He wanted to see if the back door was unlocked so he bolted around the building with the police giving chase behind me.

"Where are you going?" an officer called behind him.

"I'm going to help my mom!" King responded.

When he reached the door, he stopped. The back door was slightly ajar. Fear overcame him when he saw the kitchen chairs turned over, broken dishes, and bloody shoeprints on the tile floor. He knew there was a lot of blood somewhere.

"Don't go inside the house! Stop!" the officer shouted.

King pushed through his fear and ran inside. As he raced upstairs, he couldn't miss the bloody footprints on the stairs. He made it to his mother's bedroom. It was unrecognizable. There was blood splattered on the walls; bloody handprints and smears stained the walls. The contents of the dresser were on the floor. Her bed that was made earlier was stripped of its sheets and his grandmother's picture lay broken on the floor. He stepped into the bedroom, slipping in a puddle of blood. It was so dark and thick, he didn't immediately recognize it as blood; it didn't look real. However, he didn't see his mother. King felt someone's hand grab his shoulder and he attempted to swing to defend himself. He realized that it was an officer pulling him out of the bedroom. The officer escorted him out the back door as others went in cautiously. He was taken back to the front.

King prayed the front door would open and his mother would be standing there. When the door opened, more people rushed in and others hurried out. In horror, he watched the chaos.

"Richie! King!" Richie's mother called out.

"Over here!" Richie waved at his mother.

"What happened?" she asked frantically.

"We heard his mom screaming. It sounded like someone was killing her. I called the police, and then I called you," he explained.

"Ma'am, are you the mother of one of these boys?" an officer asked.

"Yes, this one is mine and he is our neighbor. His mother is deaf. Is she all right?" she asked.

"Let me talk to you over here, please," the officer said.

His mother walked over to speak with the officer.

They watched them closely. She began to cry and look over at the boys.

An officer walked over and asked them questions. King answered what he could and Richie answered the rest. He was in shock. The longer it took him to see his mother, the worse he felt.

They wanted phone numbers for King's relatives. He gave them Aunt Pearl's and Sonya's information. He waited for his mother's beautiful face to grace the doorway, but it never did. Patricia, Sonya, and her husband, Raymond, arrived in minutes. They lived in the area.

"King!" Raymond called out, as they searched the crowd for him. King ran over to them, hugging them tightly. "What happened?" he asked.

"Something happened to my mom. She is still in the house."

Sonya screamed out. Both Raymond and King looked in the direction of where she had looked. His mother was on a stretcher, being wheeled quickly to a waiting ambulance. Even through the white sheets that covered her small body, blood soaked through making her wounds apparent.

King broke free from Raymond and raced over to the back of the ambulance. No one stopped him. He reached her, just as she was being lifted into the back. Her battered face had several cuts and her jaw swelled. She was still breathing, but her breath was shallow. It looked as if each breath hurt her.

"Mom, I'm right here," he said.

He reached under the bloody white sheet to find her hand and she squeezed his hand as tightly as she could.

"Move back. We have to get her to the hospital," the paramedic said.

"What hospital are you taking her to?" Raymond asked.

"MCV, sir."

"King, let's go! We are going to meet them at the hospital," Raymond said.

Raymond, Sonya, and King raced to their Thunderbird. Sonya was still visibly upset. Patricia was in her car and ready to follow. On the ride to the hospital, King sat quietly, never shedding a tear. He felt as if he wanted to cry, but he couldn't.

In the waiting room of MCV were his great Aunt Pearl and her two daughters. She cried and was consoled by one of her daughters, Michelle. When she saw King, she cried even harder.

"Are you all right?" Michelle asked.

She was the youngest of Aunt Pearl's children while Loreal was the oldest. She sat in silence across from Aunt Pearl and Michelle. When Loreal saw King, she ran to him and hugged him tightly. She didn't say anything. She just held him close to her.

When Loreal was done, Michelle quickly moved in. She rubbed his head. With weak red eyes she asked, "Are you all right, King?"

"Yeah. Have you seen my mom yet?"

"No, but she's here."

"Can I see her?"

"Not until the doctor let us know it's okay to see her."

"Is she going to die?"

"We are praying that she recovers. Your mom is a strong woman; you know that. Believe me; she is fighting for her life. She has to be here with you."

"King, poor child. Did you see who did this to your mother?" Aunt Pearl asked between sobs.

"No, but I tried. When I got around the back, I didn't see nobody," King said.

He couldn't believe how close he was to seeing the person that hurt his mother. Somehow they outsmarted him. The person had to have seen him looking through the mail slot, but it didn't seem to faze them. They continued to walk calmly down the stairs.

The sound of his mother's screams echoed in his head as the horror played in darkness.

"Family of Jasmine Peterson," a doctor called out.

Everyone jumped quickly from their seats, except King. He moved slowly as he felt something rip from him, setting his stomach on fire. He knew she was gone.

"We're here. Please, tell us she is going to make it. Oh, God, please!" Aunt Pearl cried out.

"Please, follow me," the doctor said.

They followed her and another man dressed in a black suit, down the hall to a room with more chairs and tables. An eerie feeling was in that room. A bad aura hovered above them as they took their seats; Raymond was left standing.

"I'm sorry to inform you that Jasmine Peterson has passed. She suffered over fifteen stab wounds to multiple parts of her body. The most severe were the wounds to her chest. She fought her attacker. There were numerous defensive wounds on her hands and arms. We did everything we could to save her; I am so sorry for your loss. The Chaplain is here to speak with you," she said.

The doctor left the room and a nurse entered. Each one of them mourned her death in their own way. Patricia, Sonya, and Aunt Pearl mourned loudly. Loreal and Michelle sobbed quietly. Raymond shed a few tears as he tried to console Sonya, who had fallen to the floor.

King didn't say a word. He watched everyone else's pain as he stored his away.

He was sad and he was hurt. His emotions just wouldn't let him cry. He felt like yelling and hitting something, but he didn't move.

Who would want to hurt my mom?

She was kind, beautiful, and gentle. For her to die in such a brutal way was unjust. She was alive and well only hours ago. Now, she was never coming back.

She would never see her son again. Never watch me grow into a man.

Even at those thoughts, he didn't cry. Nothing happened.

That was the day King's life changed. Not only did he lose his mother, but also his innocence was taken from him. He was hardened and cold. He wanted to punish the man that killed his mother and took no regard for him. King would spend many years looking for his mother's killer and preparing himself for that day.

CHAPTER 8

After his mother's funeral, he officially moved in with Aunt Pearl. Before that, he stayed with Loreal at her one-bedroom studio. Aunt Pearl's house wasn't childproofed and she needed time to set up his new room.

King used to visit Aunt Pearl's with his grandmother. She had so much clutter in her home that it was hard to find anywhere to sit anything down. There were old magazines piled on the coffee table and too many coasters. Porcelain and glass knickknacks were placed across the house, mostly porcelain cats.

Thick plastic covered her floral designed sofa. In the summer, he sat on the floor, because he didn't want to melt on the sofa. A fan in the window of the living room and back bedrooms served as her air conditioning.

Loreal and Michelle were dropping him off at Aunt Pearl's. When they pulled up to the house, he noticed an older girl sitting on Aunt Pearl's porch. He'd never seen her before. He wanted to ask who she was, but he was sure he was soon to find out. He hadn't spoken much for a couple of weeks. He watched the girl as she watched them. Her legs sat high to her chest and her arms appeared too long for her skinny body.

"Come on, King," Michelle said. She turned to face him in the back seat of the car. She smiled at him. "My mom has a foster child staying here for a while. Her name is Starlene, but we call her Starr. You two should get along fine. She's a nice girl."

The car jerked as Loreal placed the car in park. The engine sputtered, and then the car cut off. King shook his head as the engine backfired. He was tired of being embarrassed by that old car.

He didn't respond to Michelle. He just grabbed his book bag that held the only pieces of clothing that he owned, thanks to his cousins.

Aunt Pearl appeared in the screen door, wearing a pink housecoat heavily decorated in flowers. Michelle opened the door to the car and pulled up her seat to let him out. He climbed out of the car, dragging his book bag behind him. Loreal was already halfway to the door, and he followed behind Michelle.

When they reached the girl sitting on the porch, Michelle knelt down and hugged her. She hugged her back.

"King, this is Starr. Starr this is my little cousin, King. He is going to be staying here for a while," Michelle explained.

"What's up, King?" Starr said. She flashed the most beautiful smile he'd ever seen, other than his mother's. The gap between her two front teeth didn't take away from that. Her eyes held a story, a painful one.

"What's up?" he said, throwing his head back.

"So, I guess you're going to be like my little brother, since I'm older than you are," Starr said, as she looked him up and down.

"How do you know how old I am?" he asked.

Starr stood to her feet and put her hands on her hips. She glared down at him.

"Look, boy, I am sixteen years old and I know you ain't nowhere near my age," she said.

"Sit your grown butt down," Aunt Pearl said.

Starr was unaware that Aunt Pearl was in the door. Starr quickly removed her hand from her hip and sat back down on the step. She rolled her eyes and sucked her teeth at him.

Michelle and Loreal burst out laughing. He didn't know who Starr thought she was, but she wouldn't be talking down to him or bossing him around. Her smart mouth and attitude would be a problem. He was glad that Aunt Pearl put her in her place.

"Come on in, King. I've been around here getting your room all ready for you. I know how y'all boys are and you ain't going to tear up my house," Aunt Pearl said. She held the door open for them.

She was right; she'd done some work. There was less clutter and less knick-knacks placed around the living room. She reached for his book bag and he hesitantly handed it over to her. When the book bag left his hands, he felt as if he had nothing.

"Let me show you to your room. I had the room painted just for you," she said.

King followed her down the narrow hallway and to the last bedroom on the left. She stopped at the doorway. The door was closed as were all the doors that they passed. She looked at him and smiled, showing her dentures. She opened the door and pushed him in.

"Surprise!" she said.

King walked in slowly. The room was no longer a sewing room as he remembered it.

"Thank you. I like it," he said.

"This was my sewing room. I had my sewing machine and table right over in that corner." She pointed where the bed was. "Make sure you wear shoes on this carpet, because it's full of pins. I did the best that I could to get as many of them up. I made the sheets and curtains myself. Do you like it?"

"Yes, green is my favorite color."

"I thought so. My sister, rest her soul, decorated your room in green when you were a baby." She looked to the heavens.

"I miss both of them," he said.

"I know you do. They are in a better place now, looking down over you. They are your guardian angels now, baby," she said in a shaky voice. "Now go in and get unpacked. I have something on the stove for you. I know they were over there feeding you all that fast food, because neither one of them can cook to save their lives. And, to think I raised them. They ain't learn nothing about cooking a decent meal," she said.

King was thankful for having someone step in and take care of him, but he was still numb. He wasn't happy or sad at that moment. He didn't know how to feel. Guilt set in when he thought he finally found a small piece of happiness. He was grateful for his cousins; Michelle and Loreal promised to help when they could, and so far, they had been there for him.

He walked over to the twin bed covered in green sheets and put down the book bag on the bed. The room was small, but comfortable. There was a bed, dresser, and mirror. He opened the drawers to find them filled with clothes. The first drawer contained neatly folded brand new white t-shirts, underwear, and socks. He opened the second drawer to find neatly folded shirts. He pulled out a shirt from the top of a stack to see if it was the right size. Underneath it was a plaid black and white button up. He remembered begging his mother to buy him that shirt for his birthday. He picked up the shirt and looked at it. He wasn't sure if it was the same shirt. He looked on the right sleeve to see if there was a small cigarette burn where he and Richie stole his mother's cigarettes. His eyes watered when he found the burn on the sleeve.

"Hey, Cousin," Michelle said, appearing in the doorway.

"Hey," he said, choking back tears.

He shoved the shirt back into the drawer and closed it. Michelle walked over and sat on the bed.

As he went to sit down beside Michelle, she stopped him, nudging him towards the closet.

"Look in the closet," she said.

He looked at her with suspicion. He wondered what was so important about the closet. He'd already seen the clothes that they were able to get from his old apartment.

"All right," he shrugged.

He walked to the closet slowly. He turned the gold door knob and slowly opened the door. There on the floor, he found his old toy box, with his collectible comics and action figures. Against the wall was his electric football game. His face lit up with excitement.

"Thank you!" he said, reaching into the closet to retrieve his electric football game. He pulled it out and closed the closet door behind him.

"I knew that was going to put a smile on your face. Your friend Richie told us to make sure we gave it to you. We tried to hook up that video game, too," she said, pointing to the Atari on a TV stand. "I'd been trying to get you to cheer up all this time. We were able to get some of your mother's things, too. We are going to hold on to them until you are ready for them," Michelle said.

"Man, I begged my mom for this and she was finally able to get it for Christmas. I wish I could play with my friends. Do you think I can still visit them sometimes?" King asked.

"You will see them at school. You are lucky you're still able to go to the same school. I know you are going to miss your old friends, but you are going to make new ones, too. There are a lot of little knuckleheads your age running around here," Michelle said.

King began to set up his players on the board. He thought about Christmas morning and how happy his mother was to give him that gift. A lump formed in his throat and his face began to feel warm. His heart pounded at a faster pace than normal. His spirit needed a release of the pain he felt. Warm tears filled his eyes and poured out onto his cheeks, rushing down his face. There was no stopping them. Sobs followed and echoed in the silence of the room.

Michelle quietly kneeled down beside him and rubbed his back as he cried. She didn't say a word. She allowed him to finally mourn his mother's death. Fast, heavy footsteps echoed down the hall towards the bedroom.

"Oh, my Lord. Child, are you all right?" Aunt Pearl asked. She pulled him up towards her frail body and held him in her arms. "Let it out. Only God knows your pain. Go ahead and let it out." She rocked him back in forth in her arms, encouraging him to release his pain and cleanse himself of sorrow.

Minutes later, his tears stopped and the sobs silenced. His heart closed once again. He bottled his rage and anger, saving it for the person responsible for his mother's murder. That same man had disregarded him.

He looked over at Michelle, who had shed tears of her own. She reached for him as he wiped his tears. He didn't want to be treated like a baby. He was a man in the making on a mission to hunt down and kill the man that took his mother away from him. It was a harsh realization that his life had changed and he couldn't do anything about it. Life dealt him a hand and he had to play it. Although, he felt he'd failed his mother by not being able to prevent what happened, he couldn't help but feel the overwhelming love that she had for him.

"King, you get yourself together, and then come on out so that you can eat your dinner. Come on out of there, Michelle and let that boy grieve," Aunt Pearl said, as she left the room.

"Are you okay?" Michelle asked. She wiped her face with the back of her hands.

"Yeah, I will be. Can I ask you something?" he asked.

"You know you can ask me anything."

"Do they know who killed my mom?"

"Not since the last time my mom spoke to the detective a few days ago. I am sure they are still investigating. They will contact us once they find out something. I still can't believe what they did to her. Who would want to hurt her? I have to go. If you need anything and I mean anything, call me. Even if you just want to get away from my mama, call me." Michelle gave him a tight hug and kiss on the cheek.

"Make sure you answer my call, too."

"You know I will."

He was finally alone. He picked up his electric football game and placed the pieces back in the box. The smell of fried chicken was pleasing to him. He moved faster at the thought of eating some home-cooked food.

"Are you okay?" Starr asked. She walked in and sat on the bed, twisted a braid between her fingers, and smacked loudly on gum as she waited for a response.

"Yeah, I guess," he said.

"What happened?"

"It don't matter. I'm cool now. How long are you supposed to be here?" He placed the game in his closet and sat on the other end of the bed.

"I don't know, but I'll be eighteen soon. I'm going to get my own place." She put her feet on the bed and lay back on the pillow.

"What the hell? Get your dirty shoes off my bed!" King said.

"Shut up!" She didn't move her feet.

He slapped her feet off the bed, just as Aunt Pearl came down the hall. "What are you kids doing in here? Didn't you hear me calling you? It's time to eat," Aunt Pearl called out.

Both Starr and King jumped up from the bed. She blocked them both.

"Wash your hands before you think about sitting at my table," Aunt Pearl said.

"Yes ma'am," they said in unison.

They went into the bathroom and proceeded to take turns washing their hands. King was first as Aunt Pearl stood by watching them carefully. The two of them glared at each other; Starr even elbowed him once.

Aunt Pearl had cooked fried chicken, collard greens, candied yams, and macaroni and cheese. A pitcher of sweet tea and diet Pepsi was on the table. A basket of freshly buttered yeast rolls had steam rising from them. He was in heaven.

"This is all of my favorites. This is how my grandma used to cook on Sundays," King said. He slid out a chair on the opposite side of the table from Starr. Aunt Pearl sat at the head of the cherry finish dining room table, which was set for three.

"Everything looks and smells so good, Ms. Pearl," Starr said.

"Well, thank you, child," she said. "Come on; let us say grace before the food gets cold." Aunt Pearl, Starr, and King bowed their heads and closed their eyes.

"Dear Lord, thanks for the food we are about to receive for the nourishment of our bodies. In Jesus' precious name we pray, Amen."

She bellowed Amen three more times, before ending the prayer.

King opened one eye to see if Starr was as amused by the prayer as he was. She sat quietly with her eyes closed tightly, mumbling to herself.

"Amen," Starr said.

He opened his eyes and reached for a fried chicken leg from the platter of golden fried chicken.

"Say, Amen, before you touch this food, boy," Aunt Pearl said, slapping his hand away from the platter of chicken.

"Amen, sorry," he said, pulling back his hand.

"Now let's eat," she said with a smile.

King hesitantly reached for the chicken again, that time keeping his eye on Aunt Pearl. She nodded her approval, as she loaded her plate with a heaping amount of collard greens. Starr was politely waiting for Aunt Pearl to pass her the bowl of collard greens.

"King, how does your chicken taste? It taste just like your grandmother's, doesn't it?" Aunt Pearl asked, as she bit into a golden, fried chicken leg. You could hear the crunch, and then the juiciness as her teeth sunk into the meat.

"Yes, it tastes just like Grandma's chicken. It's even pretty like her chicken," he said, with a mouthful of macaroni and cheese.

"That's right. It's her special recipe. Nobody fried chicken like my older sister. Big Mama taught her how to cook and she taught me. I was only nine years old, standing over a pan of Crisco," she said, with a small laugh. She picked up a napkin from the table and dabbed the corners of her mouth.

"My mom could cook like her too," he said. This time, when he talked about his mother, he didn't feel anger curl up his spine, but fondness as he thought about her.

"Can we talk about something else, other than dead people," Starr blurted out. As soon as the words left her mouth, she cut her eyes over at Aunt Pearl.

"Now, I know you didn't just say that. If you don't like the conversations going on in this house, just don't participate," Aunt Pearl said.

"I'm sorry," Starr said. She looked down at her plate, and stabbed her chicken with the fork.

Aunt Pearl cleared her throat and looked over at King, who was almost done cleaning his plate of food.

"Slow down. It's plenty of food here. Drink something before you choke," she said.

King swallowed hard as he forced the food down. He picked up the cup of sweet tea and drank it. He gulped down the tea as if he'd had nothing to drink for days.

"Boy, slow down. You are an animal! I am going to have to teach you some table manners. I know my dear sister taught you better than that," Aunt Pearl said. She fanned herself with a napkin.

After dinner, both Starr and King had to work together, cleaning the kitchen. Aunt Pearl's job was to cook and their jobs were to clean the kitchen after dinner.

"King, clear off the table and take out the trash. Starr, you already know you have to wash the dishes and put away the food. Don't forget to sweep the floor," Aunt Pearl instructed.

"Yes, ma'am," Starr said. "Is he going to help with the dishes, too? He ate just like we did."

She grimaced, twisting her face. From the look on her face, she didn't like washing dishes. She flashed King an evil glare behind Aunt Pearl's back, and he scowled back at her.

Aunt Pearl took a second to think about Starr's question before answering. "Do what I tell you to do. We all have to pull our weight around here. Don't worry about him," she said.

King prayed that he didn't have to wash dishes. He never had to wash dishes at home and he didn't want to start. He was fine with the chores she had given him.

"Why can't he help?" Starr asked.

Aunt Pearl walked briskly up to Starr. She placed her hand on her hip and shook her right index finger in Starr's face. "I said you were washing dishes and that's the end of it. You keep right on testing my patience, little girl, and you will find yourself right back out there in them streets. You don't want to be out in the cold, trust me. Your little grown butt better stop playing with me, little girl," Aunt Pearl said.

King smirked at Starr, who was apparently embarrassed. He got up from the table with a happy smirk, knowing that he wouldn't be put on kitchen duty with Starr. He picked up his plate and reached across for Starr's.

"Get them dishes, boy!" Starr shouted.

Aunt Pearl didn't say a word. She eyed them both and left the kitchen, shaking her head.

He picked up Starr's plate and she yanked it from him.

"Let me show you how it's done," she said nastily.

She picked up her plate and scraped the remaining food onto Aunt Pearl's plate. Then his plate was scraped onto Aunt Pearl's plate. She stacked the two clean plates on top of each other, then the plate of food on top.

"Now scrape this plate into the trash and put them on the counter so that I can wash them. If there is any food in my dishwater, you're going to pay. You got that boy?" she said.

Just then, Aunt Pearl returned to the kitchen with a thick, black leather belt in her hand. Starr and King both froze in their steps.

"Little girl, I'm the only woman in this house. I done told you about talking to him like you his mama. He's only been here one day and you are already getting on my nerves. You're not going to make no punk out of him, bossing him around like that. Now you got that!" Aunt Pearl snapped.

"Yes, Aunt Pearl," Starr answered.

King burst out laughing. Seeing Aunt Pearl scold Starr was pure entertainment for him. Starr got on his nerves and he didn't like the way she treated him.

Both Aunt Pearl and Starr looked at King strangely, as he laughed until tears fell from his eyes. When he was done, he gathered the dishes and took out the trash as he had been instructed.

Aunt Pearl checked the kitchen to ensure everything was done to her liking. After she was satisfied with their work, she sat down to watch television.

Aunt Pearl sat out a washcloth and towel on his bed, giving him a hint that it was bath and bedtime. As King ran his bath water, he noticed the bathroom smelled rather nice. He looked around and found a basket of potpourri on the back of the toilet. Just like the rest of the house, the bathroom had Aunt Pearl's floral design. The shower curtain was pink with pink and white roses. The bathroom was complete with a pink rug set, and on the wall was a picture of a field of flowers and blue skies.

Aunt Pearl insisted on knocking on the door several times, instructing King on how to properly wash.

"Make sure you scrub under your arms real good," she said. Five minutes later, "Make sure you scrub your butt last."

All he could say was, "Yes ma'am."

After his bath, he opened a fresh pack of briefs. He opened his drawer in search of the green flannel pajamas he had seen earlier. He found them and held them, as he thought of his mother. With every hour that passed, he missed her more and felt further away from her.

He put on his pajamas and climbed into bed. He felt a bit more comfortable sleeping at Aunt Pearl's house than at his cousin's house. Her home was more familiar, because he had been there many times with his grandmother and his mother.

King found himself getting more relaxed as he lay in bed. The house was quiet and peaceful. He usually went to sleep while watching television. In the darkness and quietness, all he could do was think. He thought about his mother and the direction that his life would go. At the early age of twelve, he worried about his future; a future without his mother or father. In school, he was taught that he could be whatever he wanted to be when he grew up. He used to want to be a fireman, but now, he wanted to be a killer to avenge his mother's death.

He decided that night to accept his current situation. He was with family and he wouldn't complain. He relaxed his shoulders and breathed a little easier. He fought back tears as the realization set in that this was his life at that moment. A longing for his mother would always claw at his heart, but he would learn to live with it. As he closed his eyes, he thought back to the day he lost his mother. He fought off the thoughts by saying the Lord's Prayer repeatedly, until he fell asleep.

CHAPTER 9

King missed his mother very much and wished that things hadn't come to what it did. Aunt Pearl loved him and made sure that he had everything that he needed. She cooked as if it was Thanksgiving most nights, stuffing him with homemade goodies. She allowed him to be a boy. She didn't try to keep him in the house all the time, but allowed him to stay out, until the streetlights came on. Then, he had to be in the front of the house. He was even able to stay over at friends' houses, something she didn't allow Starr to do. If Starr wanted to stay over at a friend's house, Aunt Pearl always said no. Her friends always had to go to Aunt Pearl's to spend the night.

It was Wednesday night and King went home with a fever after school. Every Wednesday night was Bible study and both King and Starr had to attend. Sunday was no exception. You had to be on your deathbed to miss a Sunday from church.

"Starr, you stay home with King tonight. Make sure at eight o'clock, you give him some more Tylenol for that fever," Aunt Pearl said. She gathered her Bible and white lace handkerchief.

"Yes, ma'am," Starr said. She flipped through the channels on their new television. Michelle had convinced Aunt Pearl to replace the floor model television with a newer model. Aunt Pearl did replace the television, but set the new television on top of the floor model.

"When am I supposed to cut off the soup?" Starr asked, without taking her eyes off the television.

"In about twenty minutes. Make sure you stir the soup. He will need a big bowl full of broth and vegetables to get better. I even put in my sister's secret ingredients," she said. As usual, she looked to the sky and shook her head in sadness at the thought of her sister no longer being here on earth.

Starr rolled her eyes.

"I'll be back soon," Aunt Pearl said.

Cable was the new addition to entertainment around the house. Before that, they watched old westerns on VHS with Aunt Pearl each night. Michelle and Loreal convinced her to make the house more kid-friendly, since King and Starr lived with her.

"Aunt Pearl?" King called out from his bedroom. He'd been asleep before Aunt Pearl left for church.

Starr watched music videos, something Aunt Pearl didn't like her to do. She was convinced that music videos were a bad influence on young people. Starr moved slowly off the sofa, with her eyes glued to LL Cool J. She heard King call out, but struggled to break her trance.

"What are you doing? Where is Aunt Pearl?" King asked, snapping Starr back into reality. He managed to get out of bed when no one came to see what he needed. He was wrapped in his blanket that trailed behind him.

"Oh, I'm sorry. I was coming." She took a good look at him and determined that being out of bed wasn't a good idea. His eyes looked weak and he swayed side to side, as if he would fall over. "Are you okay?"

"No, I'm not. I feel like shit," he said. He managed a small smile, when Starr burst out laughing.

"I have to watch my mouth around you," she said. "Come here. You look like you're about to fall over."

"I feel like it," he said. King walked slowly towards Starr, who met him halfway to assist him to the sofa.

"You know you have the flu. She said we all are going to catch it, too. So, I guess I better take care of you, because you will be doing the same for me." She let him sprawl out on the sofa. She placed his blanket on top of him.

"Let me fix you a bowl of soup. Just relax, I'll take care of you," she said. She touched his cheeks with the back of her hand, as she had seen Aunt Pearl do many times before. "Oh my God, you are burning up!"

She looked at the pink watch on her wrist and realized it was eight-thirty already. She rushed to the bathroom and opened the medicine cabinet where Aunt Pearl kept all of the medicine. She frantically searched for the Tylenol, but didn't see it. She went into King's room and found the bottle of Tylenol with a note attached telling her the dosage and time on his nightstand. Beside the Tylenol was a sandwich bag with something that looked like Vaseline and herbs. On the bag was written, "Rub on chest".

She grabbed both and rushed back to the living room, where King appeared to have fallen asleep. She shook him violently, rousing him.

"King, wake up. I have to give you your medicine," she said.

"I am," he said weakly, without opening his eyes.

Starr swallowed hard. She measured the Tylenol and placed the medicine cup to his lips. He slowly sipped the medicine. Then she opened the smelly bag, causing the odor to quickly escape. She lifted his damp shirt and began to rub the mixture on his chest. It smelled like VapoRub, but worse. What looked like herbs, really felt like dirt, as she rubbed the mixture on his skin. She held her nose with the other hand.

"Thanks," King said.

Starr went to the kitchen to fix King a bowl of soup. She was sure that was what he needed. She figured he was weak from not eating. She didn't like the way he looked; his eyes were weak and his face was flushed. As much as she enjoyed the fact that Aunt Pearl wasn't home, she really wished she was there.

She fed King each spoon of soup. After he had eaten, he went back to bed. She checked on him often to make sure he was still breathing. When Aunt Pearl returned home from church, Starr was able to finally rest.

CHAPTER 10

One night, as King was sleeping, he heard something at his bedroom window. He sat up, looked towards the window, and listened for a moment. It was pitch black in his bedroom. The only light was from the light post that dimly shone through the curtains. He heard nor saw nothing and pulled the covers back over his head. A few seconds later, he clearly heard a light tap on his window.

King looked towards his bedroom door nervously. He thought about running in Aunt Pearl's room and waking her. He looked back at the window and saw a shadow. He leaped from the bed, tripping over his sheets.

"Dummy, open the window," a voice said.

It was a familiar voice. In his panic, it took him a minute to identify the voice. He had been called dummy at least twice before bed. The only person that called him that was Starr. Fear let go of him and a sly smile spread across his face. He tiptoed over to the window and moved back his custom-made curtains. There was Starr, ducking down behind the bushes. She looked as if she was freezing.

"What do you think you're doing? Aunt Pearl is going to whoop your ass!" he said. He propped his arms comfortably on the windowsill and looked out at Starr.

"If you don't open this damn window, I'm going to kill you! Now, open this damn window, boy!" she said through clenched teeth. Her teeth chattered as her breath formed clouds around her.

"Where have you been? I know you didn't sneak out and forget how to get back in. You didn't think this dummy was going to let you in, did you?" he asked, taunting her.

"Boy, when I get my hands on you…" she said angrily.

"What are you going to do to me? You're going to have to learn to respect me, girl. I am the man of this house now. Stop calling me dummy and boy. My name is King. And, don't keep putting your hands on me, either. Not unless you want Aunt Pearl to know about you slipping out the house at night," he said.

"Okay, okay. Just let me in," she said. She folded her arms around herself for warmth, rubbing her hands back and forth up and down her arms.

King let her suffer for a few more seconds before unlatching the window lock and lifting the window to help her crawl in. When Starr was inside, he saw just why she was shivering. She had on the thinnest, shortest dress he'd ever seen.

"What are you looking at…" she started. She quickly stopped before she finished.

"Say it. I want you to," he dared.

She eyed him angrily as she grabbed his blanket from his bed and wrapped it around herself. King climbed back in bed. He didn't want to be a victim if Aunt Pearl was to awaken.

"Where were you?" he whispered.

"I went out with my boyfriend," she said.

"I hope it was worth it, because I think Aunt Pearl is up." He pulled the covers over his head and pretended to be asleep.

The hallway light came on, followed by heavy dragging footsteps. They stopped right at King's door.

"What are you doing in here, child?" Aunt Pearl asked.

King peeked from under the covers to see the action that was about to happen. Starr was so scared she didn't say a word. Her mouth was open, but she was frozen.

"Did you hear me, girl?" she asked. This time, Aunt Pearl placed her hand on her rounded hips. Her head moved with each word, causing her rollers to wobble in her hair.

"I couldn't sleep," Starr said.

"I know you couldn't, because you weren't in your bed. I wasn't born yesterday on nobody's pickle truck. I know you been sneaking out of here. Why do you think that window was locked tonight?" Aunt Pearl asked.

King continued pretending to be sleep, until Aunt Pearl eyed him suspiciously. She gave him a look that said, 'I know you're not sleep. Stop playing'.

Both Starr and Aunt Pearl looked over at King, who faked a yawn and stretched.

"King, I know you're not sleep! Did you let her in my house?" Aunt Pearl asked.

"Yes ma'am," he said nervously.

"Then, let her back out the same way she came in here," Aunt Pearl said.

"Huh?" Starr asked. She looked at both King and Aunt Pearl.

"She came through the window," King said.

"I don't care if she fell through the ceiling. Let her butt

out the way she came in. You helped her in here, now help her out," Aunt Pearl said.

"No, I don't want to leave, Aunt Pearl. I'm sorry for sneaking out," Starr cried out.

"Oh, now you can talk. Don't matter to me. Climb your butt back out my window and go wherever you just came from. I hope they have food and clothes for your behind," Aunt Pearl said.

"Please! No! I don't want to go," Starr said.

"Aunt Pearl, it's freezing outside. Look at what she has on," King said. The room fell silent, except for Starr's sniffling.

"I said, let her out the same way she came here or you can leave right behind her," Aunt Pearl said sternly.

She moved closer into the bedroom, causing both Starr and King to jump into action. They looked at each other. Starr had tears running down her face. King felt sorry for her and really didn't want to let her out of the window. He had no choice in the matter and decided to do what he was told. Unlike Starr, he had nowhere else to go.

He slowly opened the window, but not before pretending to have a hard time with the lock. They looked at each other as Starr put one leg out of the window, exposing her undergarments in the tiny dress she wore. He helped lower her down. That was when he noticed the bruise on the side of her eye. She met his eyes.

"It's okay," she said.

"Come back in thirty minutes, I'll let you back in," King whispered, and then winked at her.

Starr smiled widely. "Okay, thanks."

"Now close and lock my window. If a person doesn't knock on this front door, then they don't get in. Do you understand that? Let this be a lesson to you," Aunt Pearl said.

"Yes ma'am," he said. He pretended to lock the window.

"Good night," she said.

King climbed into bed and fought off sleep by thinking about the lesson he had learned. The lesson was not to mess with Aunt Pearl. She was old, but she wasn't stupid. She didn't tolerate anything less than respect in her house.

The house was extremely quiet. He could hear the car engines roar on the roads. Lately, when everything quieted, King found himself hearing echoes of his mother's screams. While waiting on Starr, it happened. The sounds of his mother's ear-piercing screams filled his head and left no room for him to breathe. It took him right back to that day. Then, all he could see was bloody footprints, and bloody handprints.

King closed his eyes as tightly as he could and grabbed his head with both hands. He shook his head violently as he tried to think about his friends, school and the last episode of the Flintstones that he'd seen. Good thoughts battled with the bad ones, pushing the screams and sight of blood out of his head.

The sound of his window sliding open finally snapped him back into reality. Starr lifted herself through the window and the cold air rushed in behind her, giving him a sharp sting to his sweaty body.

"Are you okay? What's wrong with you?" Starr asked, rushing over to him.

"I don't know. I keep hearing my mother's screams and seeing blood every time I close my eyes," he told her.

Starr examined him for a moment. She watched as sweat dripped down his forehead and his cheeks were flushed. His eyes bulged, giving him a wild look.

"You need to tell Aunt Pearl about that. I saw you

shaking through the window. I thought you were having a seizure or something," she said.

Starr hugged King tightly. He held her just as tight. For a moment, he felt safe in her arms. He felt that she would always be there when he needed her.

"From now on, I got your back. You don't have to worry about me being mean to you anymore. Now, you are my little brother. All we have is each other," she said.

The sound of those words was like music to his ears. He wanted so desperately to have someone in his corner.

"Family for life," King said. He lifted his head from her shoulder and offered her his hand.

She smiled and said, "Family for life, little brother." They shook on it. Starr wiped his tears with her bare hands.

"You know, we have a lot in common. I have nightmares, too." Starr told her story to King, something she'd never shared with anyone else.

"When I was fifteen years old, I was kidnapped and left for dead," she said.

"Why would someone do that to you?" he asked.

"If you are the child of a dope fiend, anything goes. My mother used to stand with a cardboard sign, begging for money. I'd sit on a turned over bucket, watching cars go by. Some stopped and gave us change or a few dollars. There was one woman who always came by with a sandwich or something to drink for me. She had small children of her own in the back seat of the car. I always made sure that I said thank you. My mother wasn't happy when we received food or water. She would sometimes cuss people out for handing us things like that. What she wanted was money for drugs," she explained.

King listened in amazement to Starr's story. He had no idea she'd been kidnapped.

"The day I was kidnapped, my mom sent me into the gas station for bottled water and I had to beg her for the money. It was summertime and it was blazing outside. We sat in the hot sun, begging for almost four hours. When I came out of the store, my mom called out to me from a car. I'd seen the car circle around a few times. There was a group of men riding around in it. I walked over to the car and my mom was in the back seat with two other men. She was crying."

"Why was she crying? Did they hurt her?" he asked.

Starr continued with her story as if he didn't say a word.

"She said she was going to ride with these guys. She owed them a little something. When she was done, she was going to come back for me. She told me to go back and wait for her. I told her that I didn't want to stand out there alone. I asked her when she was coming back."

King watched as tears slowly filled Starr's eyes and her voice became shaky.

"The driver yelled at me and said, 'Do what the fuck she said and stand your dirty ass on that corner and get my money'! He scared me, so I did what he told me to."

"Who did he think he was talking to you like that? What did your mother say?" he asked.

"She didn't say anything. She looked scared, too. I was too afraid to look back at the car, so I kept my head straight and headed back to our corner. I sat on the bucket and drank my water. It was a busy afternoon and traffic was heavy, because the races were in town. I sat there for three hours alone, collecting money. In all, I had forty-five dollars. I knew my mother would be so proud of me. I worried as time went on and my mother hadn't returned. We would usually head back to our apartment around seven o'clock, so I expected her back by then. When eight o'clock came and went, I knew something was wrong. I packed up our things and jumped on the city bus, hoping to find my mother at home, and waiting."

Starr took a brief pause, long enough to put her feet up on the bed and lie down beside King.

"I got off the bus and walked to our apartment complex. I twisted the door knob to our apartment on the first floor and the door was unlocked as usual. For some reason, my mom never felt the reason to lock it. She said that there wasn't shit in there that anyone would want. I called out for her, but she wasn't there."

King and Starr froze as they heard a sound in the house. They stopped breathing for a second. After a few moments, they realized it wasn't Aunt Pearl.

"Go ahead," King said anxiously.

"About fifteen minutes later, my mother was banging on the front door. She was covered in blood. I had never seen so much blood in my life. I just knew she was badly hurt. She kept saying that everything was fine and that she was all right. I tried checking her body for injuries, but didn't find any. My mother walked into the house as if everything was fine. I helped her to the sofa. Her left eye was swollen shut. Blood was smeared all over her shirt and shorts.

"What happened to her?" he asked.

"She told me she did something for a man and he didn't pay her. She said she stabbed him and left him in his hotel room. I couldn't believe her; I didn't understand why she would put us in danger like that. Her hands were still dripping blood, so I told her to wash her hands in the bathroom. I could tell she was high, because she nodded off just that fast."

There was a brief pause. Starr took a deep breath before continuing with her story. King waited patiently.

"There was a knock at the back door. The last thing I remembered after opening the door was a man that I'd never seen before, pulling me out the door. He pulled out a gun and told me that if I screamed, he would kill me. I woke up in the hospital all kinds of messed up. I had been beaten and he stabbed me. I was stabbed twice in my stomach, see?" Starr lifted her dress to show a scar from her belly going down into her underwear and one cut on her side.

"Damn, they messed you up! They really tried to kill you!"

"They sure did, but I didn't die. They dumped me behind a trash can in an alley and someone found me."

"This shit sounds like something off TV. I can't believe that happened to you."

"Well, it did, little brother. The cops told me what happened. My mom stole a pack from a drug dealer that was worth a lot of money on the streets. She stabbed him, smoked the dope and sold what was left of it. They held me for ransom and, of course, my mom couldn't pay up," she explained. The last time I saw her, she acted as if she didn't even know me," she said.

"Why did she let that happen to you? Didn't she know he was going to come back for his stuff?"

"Fuck her and these drug dealing fuck boys! I have something for all of them. My mother is out there somewhere smoking her life away. Because of them, I will never have children. That's why I do what I do," she said, with a sly grin.

"All I see you do is sneak in and out of windows," he said jokingly.

"Don't tell nobody I told you this, but I get these dudes hemmed up out here. I date the drug dealers who like young girls like me and take all of their money. I have even set some of them up to get locked up," she said, with a laugh.

"Aren't you scared of getting hurt if they find out what you're doing?" he asked.

"They tried to kill me once and it didn't work. I'm not scared of nothing except Aunt Pearl," she said. "Let me get to my room. Hopefully, she won't come in and kick me out again."

"Good night," King said.

Starr went to her room. King had so much on his mind he couldn't fall asleep. After hearing what happened to Starr, he understood her and respected her. She'd been through so much, but still managed to be strong. He wanted to find the same strength she had. He didn't get a chance to ask about the scar on her face, but figured she didn't let that go unpunished.

While still in bed, an idea came to mind. He figured that if Starr could avenge her attacker, he could do the same for his mother. Although, he didn't know who attacked his mother he was determined to find out. King rolled over, reached into the nightstand drawer, and pulled out a leather-bound journal that Loreal had given him to write down his thoughts and feelings. He maneuvered his curtains where the streetlight shone directly at the foot of his bed. He lay on his stomach with the journal and wrote down everything he remembered about the day his mother died. He filled three pages with the details of that day. On the fourth page, he listed suspects. With no clue as to whom or why someone would want to hurt his mother, he just named everyone he knew as suspects. He left out blood relatives, but listed everyone else he could think of. The list included his mother's friends, his friends, dope boys, addicts, and drunks.

After he had finished his list, he felt proud that he would finally do something about his mother's death. On the fifth page, he wrote his mother's name many times and drew hearts with her name in it.

I LOVE YOU MOM framed the page.

When he was done, he took the picture of his mother from his photo album and placed it between the pages. Quietly, he crept to his closet and fumbled around in the dark to find a spot to hide his journal. He buried his journal in a box filled with his old belongings.

From that day forward, Starr and King called each other brother and sister, and had each other's back. No matter what the situation was, they were there for one another. Aunt Pearl appreciated the fact that they didn't fight as much and worked together most of the time.

CHAPTER 11

King's first summer at Aunt Pearl's started off great. He celebrated his thirteenth birthday, the first one without his mother. Aunt Pearl baked him a cake and invited a few of the boys he played with in the neighborhood over for cake and ice cream. King appreciated her efforts, but he wanted to celebrate with his real friends from K.C.

He wanted to be with his friends outside of school the way that they used to be. He begged her many days to allow him to visit K.C. after school and she always opposed. She didn't allow him to ride his bike the twenty minutes to K.C., nor did she take him. It took a while for Michelle and Loreal to convince her to let him go back to the old neighborhood with proper supervision.

Richie's mom, Ms. Bowling, stayed in contact with Aunt Pearl to check on King. Ms. Bowling and Aunt Pearl developed a trusting relationship.

King packed his suitcase with enough clothes for two weeks that Aunt Pearl proudly gathered for him. He couldn't wait to see his friends. He saw them at school, but it wasn't as it used to be. At school, they couldn't talk as much as they liked. He missed walking home with them after school and talking about their day. He missed the bike rides, the store raids, and all the fun he used to have.

"Are you ready?" Michelle asked.

"I'm almost done," King said. He stuffed the last of his clothes in a suitcase.

"Are you sure you have everything? It looks like you're moving out," she said.

"I think I have everything," King said taking a last glance over his bedroom.

King's bed was made and the rest of the room was spotless. King placed the overstuffed book bag on his back. Michelle picked up the suitcase. On the way out the door, King picked up a shoebox and placed it under his arm as they left.

He and Michelle walked out to the living room where Aunt Pearl waited. She had a foil-wrapped plate in her hand. She never let him go anywhere without eating first.

"Now remember what I told you. I don't want you hanging out in the streets all day. I want you to be safe, and mind Ms. Bowling, you hear?" Aunt Pearl asked, with her free hand on her hip.

"Yes, ma'am," he said.

"I love you and call me every night before you go to bed, so that I know you're safe," Aunt Pearl said.

"Yes, ma'am," he repeated.

"Ma, he will be fine," Michelle said. Michelle brushed by the two of them, heading towards the front door.

"I love you. I'm going to miss you," she said.

King gave Aunt Pearl a big hug and kiss. He would miss her, too, but he was excited to spend time at

Richie's. They had the full two weeks planned. They would go to steal bikes, ride them downtown, and shoplift. They would go by the railroad to see the hobos and to Mike's birthday party.

Michelle dropped King off at Richie's. King stared at his old apartment as a lump formed in his throat. He wished at that moment he was returning home to his mother. She would stand at the door waiting on him as she always did. He let that imagination play out in his mind and the thought almost put a smile on his face. It was tougher than he thought it would be. As much as he tried to push the memories of his mother out of his mind the deeper, they ran. He saw the apartment and had memories of living there. He could see himself racing up the stairs and playing with his toys. He saw his mother watching television and cooking her delicious meals. He wanted to call out to her, but he knew that there wouldn't be an answer.

King placed his hand on his stomach as he became nauseated. Michelle looked over at him as she placed the car in park.

"Are you okay? I know it might be hard to come back here. If it's too much, just tell me and we can turn right back around," Michelle said in a sincere voice.

"My stomach hurts," he said, fighting back tears. He didn't realize until that moment just how much he missed home.

"It's okay, King. Whatever you need to do, just do it," she said.

With that said, King opened the door and vomited outside the car. He let go some of the tears that welled in his eyes, too. After a minute, he felt better. Michelle allowed him that time without prying or pushing him.

As King's head hung out of the door of the car, he could hear Michelle fumbling around in the car. She unlatched his seatbelt right as he heaved again with so much force that he almost fell out the car. He caught himself with the door as she reached over and rubbed his back.

After a few minutes, Richie ran outside to greet them. He ran to the passenger side of the car.

"Eww . . . did you do that?" Richie asked, as he stepped over the large puddle of vomit in between the two cars.

"He's fine now," Michelle called out from the driver side.

King sat back in his seat and breathed in and out. He felt much better as he won the fight of blocking out the darkness that invaded his mind.

"Are you okay?" Richie asked.

"I think so. I need to go in the house," King said.

King slowly stepped out the car, grabbed his book bag, and the shoebox he placed with him in the front seat. Richie moved back to let him out, so that he didn't step in the vomit. He slammed the door.

"Don't slam my door!" Michelle called out.

King and Richie waited for Michelle on the sidewalk. Three men were headed towards them, just as Michelle stepped out of the car.

"What's up, shawty?" one of the men asked.

Michelle ignored them and didn't turn in his direction.

"Oh, you too good to talk to me?" the man asked.

He walked closer to the car, dragging his three sizes too big jeans behind him. He was twisting a section of his afro between his fingers.

Michelle continued to ignore the man. She closed and locked the doors to her car, and then she walked to the apartment with King and Richie closely behind. King kept his eyes on the man. He'd seen all too often how aggressive and disrespectful men could be to women.

"Fuck you then, bitch," the man called out behind them.

"Fuck you!" King called out.

Michelle yanked King by the arm, dragging him into the apartment.

Once they were inside, she said, "You must want to go back home? You can't come around here talking like that. These people will hurt you, King," she said.

"I'm not going to let nobody disrespect my family. I don't care who it is," King said.

Michelle looked at him. "In case you didn't know, I can handle myself. And, I know that you are fully aware that a hard head makes a soft behind. Remember that," Michelle said.

King sucked his teeth at her embarrassing remark in front of Richie.

"What's going on? I know King isn't talking smart, is he?" Ms. Bowling asked. She wiped her hands on a dishtowel before she hugged King.

"One of K.C.'s finest tried to talk to me," Michelle said.

"Don't waste your time on none of those boys out there. They are either heading to prison or the grave. You are much too pretty and smart to be wasting your time like that," Ms. Bowling said.

"Here, and behave yourself," Michelle said. She handed King the suitcase. She dug in her handbag and pulled out a white envelope.

"This is money, just in case he wants something. Call my mom if you need anything," Michelle said.

"I sure will, but he will be just fine," Ms. Bowling said.

Michelle gave King a big hug. They all followed her to

85

the door and outside to make sure she made it to her car safely. The group of men was gone. She started her car and pulled off, and they went back in the house.

"Let's go upstairs," Richie said, picking up King's suitcase and carrying it up the stairs.

King followed Richie to his room. Something he'd done numerous times. This was the first time since the day the walls cried. The hair stood up on the back of King's neck as Richie opened his bedroom door. The longer he was around K.C., the stranger he felt.

"Man, how does it feel to be back around K.C.?" Richie shouted. He formed his fingers in a way that formed a K and C. "You missed everything when you moved."

King placed his book bag on Richie's bed and sat back on the bed. It wasn't long before he remembered the last time he was in Richie's room. Instead of vomiting, his skin crawled. The hairs on the back of his neck were still standing at attention.

"It doesn't feel right anymore. I feel all sick and shit," King said. He rubbed his stomach.

"That's because of what happened. Tomorrow, I bet you'll feel much better. You'll forget about it," Richie said. He turned on the television.

King knew he would never forget. In order for him to enjoy the next two weeks, he would have to try to push those thoughts far in the back of his mind, and force a smile on his face every day. He knew he would have to walk past his old apartment. He planned not to look at the door at all and walk right down the sidewalk, as if it wasn't there.

"So, how is it living with your aunt? It seems like we can't talk on the phone without her saying we running up her phone bill," Richie said.

They laughed.

"That's how she is. She even thinks that I ran up her electric bill by holding open her refrigerator door," King said, laughing hysterically.

Richie stood and walked to the door. He poked his head out and looked out into the hallway. He slowly closed the door behind him.

"Did you bring it?" Richie whispered.

"It's right here in my shoebox," King said. He reached for the shoebox.

Richie stood over King on the bed and waited anxiously. King opened the box and revealed a pair of black, shiny dress shoes. He reached inside and pulled out a bag of marijuana.

"Do you think Starr knows you stole from her stash?" Richie asked.

"She don't think I know where her stash is. I took this a week ago and she still ain't said nothing," King said.

"Good, because we gon' get high!" Richie said with excitement.

CHAPTER 12

The next morning King and Richie were up and out the door. It was warm and humid. They went straight to Alonzo's apartment, passing the early birds on the corner on their way. Richie knocked on the door and Alonzo immediately opened the door fully dressed.

"What's up?" King said.

"What's up, King? Long time no see," Alonzo said.

He was glad to see Alonzo. It was nice to see his old rival. Alonzo sent his condolences through Richie when his mother passed, but it was the first time they'd seen each other since then.

"Is your mama home?" Richie asked in a whisper.

"She left out early this morning, something about going downtown to do some shopping. So, you know she gon' be gone for a while," Alonzo said.

"Then, let us in," King said.

King and Richie rushed inside. They stopped short of the doorway and looked around.

"Where did y'all get all this new furniture?" Richie asked.

"Don't touch shit and don't sit on shit," Alonzo said.

The apartment was laced. There was no longer raggedy "hand me down" furniture. There was an all-white leather three-piece living room suit, marble top coffee and end tables. In the middle of the floor looked to be white fur draped over it. Beautiful paintings hung from the concrete walls and it smelled like vanilla. Two tall gold vases set in corners of the room. The plastic runner that they stood on ran from the front door to the kitchen. Nobody dared to move.

"This shit is tight!" King said.

"She been letting some of K.C.'s finest handle their business up in here. So, they look out for her," Alonzo said.

"Damn! I ain't never seen nothing like this. I was just over here last week," Richie said.

"I know. It happened so fast. I'm not feeling that shit. They think they running shit up in here," Alonzo said.

"Did y'all bring it?" Alonzo asked.

Richie looked at King.

"I got it," King said.

They followed Alonzo upstairs to his bedroom and then watched him open his bedroom window. He left out the room and returned with a wet towel. He closed the door and placed the wet towel at the bottom of the door. He then lit incense as King and Richie watched. That was their first time smoking weed.

"You have to do all of that to smoke some weed?" Richie asked.

"If you don't want to get caught," Alonzo said. When he was done securing the room, he said, "I have something special to go with that weed."

"What?" King asked.

Alonzo pulled a small baggie with white powder out of his pants pocket. He held it up for them to see.

"Cocaine? Man, I ain't trying to get that damn high," King said. His idea of smoking weed and getting high for the first time was backfiring.

"I've seen plenty of people do it like this. Oh, y'all too scared to try it?" Alonzo said.

King didn't want to show his fear, so he handed the sandwich bag of weed to Alonzo. He looked over at Richie and he was sweating. Alonzo took the bag and rolled four joints. King watched as he filled three with weed and the fourth with weed and the cocaine. King took notes.

"Here, let's smoke these first and save this for last," Alonzo said, handing each of them a joint. He lit his and handed the lighter to Richie, who repeated what Alonzo did. Richie gave the lighter to King and he did the same. The room filled with white, choking smoke. King mimicked Alonzo's gestures.

"You have to pull it and hold it, and then let it out," Alonzo said, blowing smoke through his nose.

After the first pull, King choked hard. Smoke filled and burned his lungs and he beat his chest to relieve the pain. Richie and Alonzo laughed at him.

"You hitting it too hard. Just inhale it and blow it out," Alonzo said.

After the burn was over, King tried again. That time, he didn't choke and Alonzo gave a nod of approval. Richie had a few choking episodes where he had to be hit in the back a few times. The more he pulled on the joint, the smaller it became. It wasn't long before King felt the high. A sensation of feeling light and floating, slowly took effect. He felt as if things happened in slow motion.

The thick smoke burned his eyes, so he rubbed them. When he opened them, they felt tight.

King didn't want the joint to end, because he didn't want to smoke the laced one.

It wasn't long before his joint was burned down to his fingertips and he had to put it out. Alonzo held the lighter to the fourth joint.

"*POW! POW!*"

Gunshots rang out. King's hearing was amplified, because it sounded like he was in the same room as the shots. His body felt heavy as he slid down onto the floor where Richie and King were already crouching.

"They shooting!" Richie said.

"It sounds like it's right outside the window," Alonzo said.

"*BOOM! BOOM!*"

Alonzo crawled on all fours to his closet. He rummaged around and returned with a black handgun.

"Where did you get that?" King asked.

"I found it in the bushes. Stop asking questions and stay down," Alonzo said.

"*POW! POW! POW!*"

"Shit!" Richie mumbled, with his hands over his ears.

Everything was in slow motion. The gunshots and their conversation swirled around in King's head. After waiting a few more minutes to see if any more shots were fired, they got up from the floor. Alonzo tucked the handgun in the small of his back and pulled his shirt down over it. All three of them rushed down the stairs and out the front door. The sunlight blinded King.

"Damn your eyes are red!" Richie said to King.

"For real? Yours are too," King said.

"You know we can't go back to my house until we come down off this high," Richie said.

No one was outside except a few others that came out to see what was going on. None of the dealers that were out earlier were outside now.

"That shit just blew my high. I still have one left. Y'all coming?" Alonzo asked.

King and Richie looked at each other.

"Naw, we gotta get back to my house before my mama come looking for us," Richie said.

"Man, I knew you were scared," Alonzo said. He shrugged his shoulders and said, "More for me then."

King and Richie walked around the corner to Mike's house. Mike filled them in on the latest shootings and drug wars. He always knew what went on in the hood. There they ate and kicked back until they felt like themselves again.

～～

The two weeks at Richie's went by fast. It was as if King hadn't missed a beat when he left K.C. Things were the same. The same dealers graced the street corner; all of his friends still lived there and did the same things as when he left. He needed to reconnect with his friends and get over some of his anxiety of going back to where he lost his mother.

Each day he walked past his old apartment, it affected him less and less. When he felt himself tunneling, he redirected his attention to something else. King felt stronger each day as he thought about how hard it was for him the first day he returned to the neighborhood and saw his old apartment.

King and Richie got dressed to meet Alonzo, Mike, and Eric to go see the hobos by the railroad tracks. There was a loud banging on the door; they could hear it upstairs in the bedroom. They continued to get dressed until they heard Richie's mom scream, "No!"

Richie rushed downstairs with his right sleeve half way off followed by a fully dressed King. When they reached the bottom of the stairs, they saw Mike and Eric with blank faces standing at the front door. Richie's mom was crying.

"What happened?" Richie asked. He struggled to put on his shoes.

"Man, we went to get Alonzo. The police and ambulance were at his house. His mom was outside screaming, and then she passed out. Then, we ran over here to get you," Eric said.

"Did you see Alonzo?" King asked.

"Naw, but they were just loading somebody in the ambulance. I think it was Alonzo," Mike said.

"Oh, my God! I have to see what's going on! I have to check on my sister!" Richie's mom said. She went into the kitchen to retrieve her keys from the key rack. "Lock up the house. Watch your sister and don't leave this house until I get back!"

Six hours later, Richie's mom returned with the worst news a teenager could hear. Alonzo accidentally shot himself in the chest. The doctors tried to save his life, but he passed away during surgery. Richie immediately broke down. His mother consoled him as they both sobbed. King was calm and reserved while he processed the news.

He'd never lost a friend. It felt different from when his grandmother and mother died. There was a different bond, a brotherhood amongst his friends. It felt like he lost a brother and best friend. King felt disconnected after Alonzo's death. The harsh reality of K.C. signified death and pain for King. He'd had enough as he felt himself lose grip of reality and freefall into darkness.

CHAPTER 13

Growing up as a teenage boy at Aunt Pearl's house was challenging at times. If he had to complain about anything, it would be that he had to attend every Bible study and Sunday church service. On Bible study night, he could convince Aunt Pearl that he had too much homework to attend church. On Sunday, there were absolutely no exceptions. If he played sick, she would make him go to church to go to the altar for prayer.

Starr on the other hand, had a much more difficult time than King did. She and Aunt Pearl seemed to fight tooth and nail most of the time. Starr wanted to hang out in the streets and do things her way, but Aunt Pearl had rules in her house. The two of them loved each other, even when they were at odds. Starr appreciated everything that Aunt Pearl did for her and tried to teach her, but Starr was too stubborn to listen. It was Starr's way or no way at all which turned out to be one of her biggest problems.

The only thing Aunt Pearl asked them to do outside of following her rules was to finish school. Starr couldn't even do that. She dropped out of high school in the twelfth grade, because she felt that her classmates were childish. She found herself in many fights that resulted in suspensions. Aunt Pearl was very disappointed, but decided that she would let that battle be hers; they saw her shed tears for the first time. Starr promised to go to night school to get her GED and she did.

King did great in school. He made good grades and was a star player on the high school football team. During one of the Friday night football games, he noticed a chocolate beauty named Maya. She was dressed in a short cheer skirt and v-style top. She wasn't skinny like the other cheerleaders. She was thicker than the other girls. King liked her thickness and her smooth dark skin.

Maya was known for being bourgeois and had ways that most people would consider "stuck up". She didn't date any of the boys at her school and made it clear anytime one of them tried to ask her out. She kept a small circle of friends and stayed out of most high school drama. King already knew that Maya didn't date and he didn't want to be rejected.

After the football game, he and Maya waited for their rides in front of the school. There were a few other students waiting around. King sat on the bench and watched as Maya paced back and forth on the sidewalk. It was cold outside and she still had on her cheerleading outfit and tights. King nervously bounced his leg as he contemplated if he should even try to approach her. There were only a few students around and they didn't seem concerned with him. If she was to reject him, it wouldn't be that many witnesses.

King watched Maya shift back and forth on her feet. Each time the wind blew, her cheerleading skirt flew up, giving him a peek at her spanks. A vehicle waited to turn into the school's parking lot and there were only five of them outside. He prayed that the car wasn't there to pick up Maya as he worked up the courage to ask for her phone number. When the car stopped a few feet away from her and she didn't move, he knew it was now or never.

He wiped his sweaty palms on his sweat pants as he thought about the words he would say to her. He'd seen her in action and wanted to come at her correct. Somewhere deep down he knew she wanted to talk to him, too. He caught her smiling at him when she thought he wasn't looking. He also noticed that when he took a bad hit in a game she would seem more concerned than the other cheerleaders would. She looked as if she wanted to run out on the field to make sure that he wasn't hurt. When he stood to his feet, she would be the loudest one cheering him on. There had to be something there; he just had to see for himself.

King cleared his throat loudly. Maya looked back at him and did a double take when she saw that it was King. She looked back at him and smiled. That was all he needed to get off the bench, leave his nerves and walk over to her.

"Hey, Maya. You look cold over there," King said. He unzipped his coat and removed it.

"Yes, it's cold out here. My locker jammed, so I couldn't change my clothes," Maya said.

She looked him directly in his eyes as she spoke to him. King felt as if she looked through to his soul. They stared at each other for a moment, gazing into each other's eyes.

97

"Here, put this around you." He placed his jacket around her shoulders.

"Thanks. This is so sweet." She smiled at him.

Things went much better than he expected. He lowered his shoulders and breathed a sigh of relief. She smiled and talked to him.

"Where's your boyfriend? He should be out here keeping you warm," he said.

"I don't have a boyfriend. Not until you came over here," she said.

"So, what are you saying?"

"What took you so long? I've been waiting on you to notice me."

"You were waiting on me to notice you? You know I've liked you since last year. All I ever saw you do was shoot every guy down that approached you. I wasn't going out like that."

"I did that for you."

"For me? How come you never said anything?"

"My mother taught me to be a lady and let the man come to me. So, I've been waiting for you." She moved closer to him, turning her body towards him. He wrapped his arms around her.

King laughed loudly. He couldn't believe that she waited for him to make the first move. He kicked himself for waiting so long to talk to her.

"What's funny?" she asked, lifting her head to look at him.

"So, does this mean I can have your number?" he asked.

"You can have whatever you like, King."

She placed her head against his chest as he held her.

"Do you need a ride home? I think that is my sister pulling up," King said.

A car pulled in slowly. King waved his hand to get Starr's attention.

"No, my dad is on the way," she said. She stepped away and removed his jacket.

"Keep it. I don't want my girl out here freezing," he said.

"Now I'm your girl?" she asked. "I don't remember you asking me to be your girl." She placed her hand on her hips.

"Do you want to be my girl?"

"Yes, I do."

"You're mine now." He hugged her tightly. Starr laid on the horn. King waved her off.

"And, you are mine. Don't try to play me, because I'm not that girl. You have one time and that's the last time. Do you understand?"

"What about you? All the dudes you have at you; I'm the one that needs to worry."

Starr stepped out of the car and rudely interrupted. "Let's go, boy. I have a date tonight."

"I'm coming. Give me a minute," he said. He looked down at Maya and kissed her. She kissed him back.

"Here, call me tonight," she said. She handed him a folded piece of notebook paper. He opened it and smiled.

"I'm glad you said something first, because I was nervous as hell," she admitted.

They hugged again. King didn't want to leave her, but he knew that if he didn't leave he would be walking home.

A pickup with a loud engine pulled behind Starr.

"I have to go. Call me when you get home," Maya said.

She walked away with King's jacket still around her shoulders. He watched her get into the truck, before he got in the car with Starr. His heart was dancing in his chest as he anxiously waited to get home. Something about her made him want to spend the rest of his life with her. Now he had two things to accomplish. Win Maya's heart and avenge his mother's death.

CHAPTER 14

Ten years later

King married the love of his life, Maya and they were expecting their first child together. After high school, Aunt Pearl gave him an ultimatum. He could go to college or he had to take a trade at one of the nearby technical centers. He chose to go to truck driving school, which she gladly financed. There he received his CDL and shortly after, was hired by a trucking company. He made a decent living there, supporting his wife and helping Aunt Pearl.

King sat in the hallway of the courthouse. There were limited seats outside of the courtroom as more people filed in. Attorneys dressed in their expensive suits and carried name brand briefcases. They spoke with their clients in private. It was early and he could already tell that the docket was full for the morning.

An older woman walked past King and stood against the wall with what looked like her grandchild. The young girl's head hung low and she didn't look to happy to be there. The older woman held her purse close to her body. She wore a tired look on her face.

"Ma'am, you can sit here," King said. He stood to his feet, offering the woman his seat.

"Thank you," the woman said. She quickly took the seat and smiled politely at King.

"No, problem," King said. He returned the smile, and then stood against the wall.

King looked at his watch. The attorney that he hired wasn't there yet and he began to worry.

"King, is that you? What are you doing here?" Ms. Doris asked. "I thought you were on the road."

King looked up, and there was Ms. Doris, the receptionist at his job.

"Good morning, Ms. Doris. What are you doing here?" King asked.

"I asked you first."

"I'm here for my sister."

"I just need to pay for a traffic ticket. I'm getting older and my driving isn't what it used to be. My daughter has threatened to take my license and keys from me. She even drove me here today. I plan to retire soon, but until then, I am doing just fine for myself. When I retire, I plan to run her all over town, since she is so eager to be my chauffeur."

"You have to be careful on the road, Ms. Doris. I've seen you drive," King teased.

Ms. Doris playfully tapped him on the arm. "I thought for sure you were out on the road this week. I didn't expect to see you until Wednesday."

"My schedule changed so that I can be in town for the birth of my daughter," he said.

"That is so nice of Mr. Brown to change your schedule like that. You know he is as rigid as they come," she said.

"Yes, I know. I plan on going back to my schedule, once I know my wife and baby are okay for me to go back on the road," he said.

"You are such a good young man. I wish there were more responsible young men like you. Well, I'll be seeing you around," she said.

"See you later, Ms. Doris," King said.

After waiting another five minutes, he decided to go outside for a smoke before the trial began. He walked outside the courthouse, down the numerous steps, and on to the sidewalk. He lit a cigarette and paced up and down the street. When he was done, it was time.

King sat in the courtroom, praying that Starr would be granted bail; one of many times that Starr found herself behind bars. She faced assault and battery charges after a fight with her boyfriend and another female. It was early and her case was first on the docket. The courtroom was full of people. He looked across the courtroom at a short, stocky man that stood with the attorney that he hired to defend Starr. He was supposed to meet him twenty minutes before. He never met her new beau, but he was sure that was he. She described him just the way he looked. The tattooed, baldhead was a dead giveaway.

Mr. Berman caught King's gaze and motioned for him to join the meeting. Standing to his feet, King straightened his black, double-breasted suit. He walked slowly over to join the two men that seemed to be in deep conversation.

"Good morning, Mr. Peterson," Mr. Berman said, extending a small, frail hand.

King accepted and firmly shook his hand.

"You can call me, King," he said.

"King, this is Jose Hernandez, my client's boyfriend," Mr. Berman continued.

"What's up, man?" Jose said in a thick Spanish accent.

"What's up?" King said.

Jose was dark-skinned and didn't appear to be Hispanic. You wouldn't have known until you heard his name or he spoke. King never knew Starr to date Hispanics, but it was clear he had money, and Starr only dated men with money. It didn't really matter how he earned it, as long as he had it and was willing to spend it on her.

"Starr told me she had a brother. Too bad we had to meet this way. I appreciate you hiring the lawyer and everything, but I will take care of this. It's my fault she is in trouble," Jose said.

"The lawyer is already paid for. I have no problem taking care of my family," King said.

Jose reached into his back pocket and pulled out an envelope. This is the fee you paid this man. I take care of my own too," Jose said.

King didn't reach for the envelope. Mr. Berman watched both men in anticipation.

"You keep that. Knowing Starr, she may need you to help her again," King said.

"Okay, next one on me," Jose said. He placed the envelope back in his pocket. He looked over to Mr. Berman.

"The woman she assaulted isn't willing to testify," Mr. Berman stated.

"Why is she locked up?" King asked.

"When police arrived, Jose was the one with scratches. Also, Starr was very uncooperative with police and continued her aggression towards Jose in police presence."

"I didn't want to press charges against her. I guess I

didn't have to. The fight was over my ex-girlfriend. She came to my house and Starr lost it. It was all my fault," Jose said.

The judge entered the courtroom and King and Jose quickly found a seat. They ended up sitting side by side on the second row with Jose closer to the aisle. Mr. Berman straightened his suit jacket and walked briskly to the front of the courtroom. He placed his briefcase on the table.

From the right side of the courtroom, a door opened and they saw Starr being escorted by a deputy. She wore the blazer and skirt that Michelle sent for her. Her hair was braided to the back in a single French braid. Her appearance was a far cry from the last time he saw her.

She walked slowly with her head down. When she was alongside Mr. Berman, she lifted her head and looked straight ahead at the judge.

King wanted her to know he was there. He willed her to look back, but she didn't. After a few seconds, he thought that maybe it was a good thing that she didn't see him and Jose sitting side by side, as if they were friends, because they weren't. Just like the rest of the men in Starr's life, they all came and went, just as fast as she was done with them.

The judge granted Starr's bail despite the fact that the prosecution objected. Mr. Berman did the job he was paid for and that was to bring Starr home. King looked at Jose, who had the widest smile on his face. There was no doubt that he was happy to have Starr back home.

After Starr's hearing, Mr. Berman, King, and Jose met in the hallway.

"Thank you, Mr. Berman. She's coming home," King said. He shook his hand.

"No problem. I have some things to finish up here. I will be talking to you soon," Mr. Berman said.

He left King and Jose alone. King didn't have anything to say to Jose. He just walked away.

"King," Jose called out.

King stopped and turned towards Jose slowly. "What?" King asked.

"Starr is going home with me. If she wants, I will bring her home later. The bondsman said she would be released in a couple of hours," he said.

King narrowed his eyes at Jose. He didn't like him. His arrogant attitude was enough, and his controlling ways started to rear its ugly head.

"I already took care of that," King said.

"Yeah, I know. Your bondsman wanted me to let you know. It was nice to finally meet you," Jose said.

"I'm not sure if I can say the same," King said, walking away.

King knew how to pick his battles. Jose was a battle to be fought another day. Starr would have to face him sooner or later. Just as the other men she dated, he would be taken to the bank or prison.

King walked out the courthouse and to his car. He checked his cell phone where there was a missed call from Aunt Pearl. She called from the assisted living facility where she opted to live. Against everyone's will, she refused to be a burden on any of them. There she had a nurse; someone to cook, and clean for her when needed. She wouldn't hear of it. She felt they were all too young to be worrying about her and had their own lives to live.

King dialed her back. "Hi, Aunt Pearl," King spoke into the phone.

"Hi, baby. How is everything going?" she asked.

"She should be home in a couple of hours. I've arranged everything."

"That's good. I don't know what that girl would do without you. She has me all worried over here. Talk to her, King; I've done everything I could to keep that girl out of trouble. It's those drugs her mama was doing. Done messed that girl's head up."

"Don't worry about it. I'll take care of everything. Did you get those flowers I sent you?"

"Yes, I did and thank you. Stop sending me all this money. I done told you I don't need it. Everything I need, I have. I'm going to get robbed."

"Nobody's messing with you Aunt Pearl, you know that. I just want to make sure you can buy whatever you want when you need it."

"I'm just fine. You just keep being a good ole boy; that keeps me happy. I love you and tell Starr to call me."

"I love you, too. She'll call you when we get back to the house, I promise."

"Oh, I want to come by the house next weekend. I want to see how the house is holding up."

"I'll pick you up."

He already knew why she wanted to go to the house. Every so often Aunt Pearl would ask to stay over on the weekends. She would spend hours in her bedroom with the door closed. One day, King was curious as to what she did in there all alone. He saw her hiding money under her mattress; the money he sent her every month. He didn't say anything about what he saw. He just continued to send her flowers and money every month.

CHAPTER 15

After leaving the courthouse, King had an hour to meet Gooch at a local gun range. Gooch was Richie's uncle who was known for his wild-west style of handling situations back in the day. He was best known for the quiet ways he handled things. Grim Reaper was what most people called him. He was a hit man who never missed a target. King sought him out years before to help him with the situation with his mother. Gooch told him that he was too young to offer his help. Now a man, Gooch knew he was ready.

King pulled into the parking lot. It was still early, but cars packed the lot. He turned off his phone so that all calls would go to voicemail. He didn't want anyone to know what he was up to, especially Maya. If she knew that he planned to murder his mother's killer when he found out who he was, she would leave him or try to talk him out of it. Only a few knew this side of him. He waited so long for Richie to plug him with his uncle, Gooch. Richie didn't totally agree with King's motives and he made it known.

He requested and received the police report from the police station. After reading the report, he was no closer to figuring out who killed his mother than he was before reading it. It only angered him more reading the gory details. The medical examiner's report showed a diagram of her wounds. There were so many marks on the paper that it sickened him. There were defensive wounds, which meant she fought her attacker. There was evidence that she was also beaten. He was never privy to the details of his mother's death and it was best that he didn't know. Hearing her cries for help was enough for him.

One thing stuck out in the report. A witness stated that he saw a young man running from the area. A very vague description was given; black male, late teens or early twenties. That described most of the guys from the neighborhood.

Gooch came from out of nowhere to King's car and leaned on the side of the car. He got out of the car.

"What's up, Gooch? I didn't see you out here," King said.

"What's good, my man? You weren't supposed to. Lesson number one," Gooch said in his deep, rough voice. He pulled out a pack of cigarettes and lit one. "If I would've lit this before making my presence known, then you would have smelled the smoke and looked around."

"Okay, I see that."

"I remember hearing about what happened to your mother. I can understand why you want to kill the person who did it. Richie said that you didn't know who was responsible for it. Is that right?"

"Yes, I don't know. All I remember was a man walking real slow down the stairs, but I didn't see his face. I know that the person knows who I am. Why didn't he run?"

"You were a little boy back then, so you may have missed something. I inquired, but came up with nothing. You know, you could just let me handle this."

"I want to handle this myself. I just want to be as skilled as you are and not get caught."

"Okay, so you want me to teach you how to kill a ghost?"

"I want you to teach me how to kill the man that killed my mother. Trust me, I've been doing some research, too." King handed him a list of names on a sheet of paper.

"What is this?" Gooch asked, holding the paper as if it was diseased.

"It's a list of possible suspects in my mother's murder. I want you to look into it for me and see what you can come up with. It's only five names on the list now. Just try to remember the people from around the way, and you shouldn't have any problems figuring out who each person is," King explained.

Gooch looked the paper over. He folded it and tucked it in his pocket. "You have heart. If you didn't, I wouldn't be wasting my time with you. I'll do what I can to help you find out who did it. Have you ever fired a pistol before?" Gooch asked, blowing smoke through his nose.

"Yeah, I fired off a few times," King said.

"But you ain't got no bodies. I ain't here to show you how to fire off a few rounds. I'm Gooch. I'm going to show you how to kill. I didn't get this age by just firing off some rounds. You have to make each bullet count. Each misfired shot is a shot at your head. That's how you have to think about it. Shoot to kill. Fuck all that shooting in the legs and chest, headshots every time unless you are trying to send a message. But that's not what you came to me for."

"Come on, Gooch, why are you trying to school me in the parking lot? Let's get inside for this target practice."

"This was your idea. I have real targets. If you ain't ready for this, I understand." Gooch threw his cigarette to the ground and stepped on it. He then picked up the cigarette and placed it in his pocket.

King was confused. He didn't want to hurt innocent people. He wanted to avenge his mother's death and finally move on with his life. A human for target practice wasn't in the plan.

"I wanted to work on my shot. That's why I wanted to come to the range. What are you trying to do?"

"Look, son, you came to me. I didn't learn to kill by shooting at the damn range. Blood don't spill at the range. You can't watch a man die in there." He pointed at the building.

"I know, but I don't want to hurt innocent people. One body is all I want."

Gooch laughed and began to sniff and rub his nose. "I got my head clear today to come down here and show you how I get down. I can go in here and babysit your ass or I can show you how to kill. It's up to you. I have work to do and money to get. The best way for you to learn is hands-on. You can't learn this shit in there or in a book. I'm Gooch, the Grim Reaper. They run and hide when they see me coming."

King leaned back on the car and thought about what he was about to do. He knew that if he rolled out with Gooch, there was no turning back. One kill was one thing, but to be part of more was another.

"I have so many bodies, I stopped counting years ago. The war made me this way. I went over there to fight for my country and came back fucked up. I did things over there that I wouldn't share with nobody. The government and the dope got me. All that made me the beast that I am," Gooch said.

"I feel you. That's why I came to you," King said.

"I'm going to show you how to do this and walk the streets like I do," Gooch said. "I'm not a teacher, so all I can do is show you."

"I want to test this heat I just got my hands on. I'm going in."

"A'ight, let me see what you got, young man."

King and Gooch went inside. After an hour of instruction from Gooch, they left. He showed him how to make only headshots. It was a start towards King's plan to execute his mother's killer.

CHAPTER 16

Starr and Jose pulled into the driveway of his home. They argued the entire fifteen minutes home. The car jerked as he came to a complete stop and Starr looked over at him in disgust. Jose put the car in park and removed the keys from the ignition, placing them in his pocket. His pit bull dogs, Killer and Moe raced to the six-foot, chain link fence, barking with excitement. She watched them jump up and down on the fence.

"You know you fucked up, right?" Jose said, with a thick accent. Whenever he was excited or upset, his English suffered. She looked out at the dogs as he spoke.

"I fucked up? What about your ex-girlfriend showing up, just when I was supposed to be leaving for the weekend?" she asked.

Jose sat stiffly as Starr stared at him. Three seconds later, the back of Jose's hand made contact with Starr's face. The impact sent her head flying towards the window. Her head hit with such force that her vision blurred. Her senses were off during the first few moments of his attack, preventing her from defending herself.

Jose struck blows to her face and stomach. Finally, Starr was able to get her bearings. She placed her back against the door and lifted her legs to deliver kicks to his face and head. He struggled with the powerful blows from her heel. She unlocked the door and slid onto the pavement on her back. As soon as she was out of the car, she jumped to her feet ready to fight.

Jose exited the car from the driver side holding the side of his head. As he moved closer to Starr, she saw why he held his head. There was a huge gash on the side of his head where his tribal tattoo was. She'd kicked him with everything she had and put a hole in his head.

"Bitch! I'm going to kick your ass!" Jose yelled. He continued to move around the car closer to Starr. The dogs barked fiercely and bit at the fence.

"Fuck you!" she shouted. Starr quickly walked down the driveway toward the street.

"Where do you think you're going? Get back here!"

"I'm leaving. I'm tired of this shit!"

Jose's demeanor quickly changed. He threw his hands up in defeat. He quickly walked behind her.

"I'm sorry! Don't leave me! Look what you did to me! I love you," he said.

Starr stopped in her tracks when she heard the magic words. She turned on her heels to face him. She had to put an end to it once and for all. Her leaving at that moment would throw a wrench in her plans. As much as she wanted to run, she knew she had to finish the job.

"Why should I stay?" she asked.

"I love you, Starr. Sometimes you make me angry and I just can't control my anger. The police are all in my business now. You know better than anyone that I don't need that around here. Are you trying to get me locked up or something?"

"Of course not; I wasn't the one who called the police. You need to check home girl."

"Don't leave me, please. I promise you, I won't hit you again."

"I know you won't," she said under her breath.

She hesitantly walked back up the driveway toward the house. She examined his wound. The very deep gash oozed blood.

"You said that the last time you hit me," she said.

"This time, I promise. Please, baby, don't go," he begged.

"This is the last time. The next time I'm leaving for good!"

"Okay, baby. I promise." He wiped the blood from his face. "Can you help me clean this up?"

"Sure, but this is it, Jose."

Jose led Starr to the house. Before they went inside, she looked around and saw no one. No one came out to see what the commotion was about. No one asked if she needed help. That was because everyone was terrified of Jose. No one dared to interfere in his business, not even when he shot a man on his lawn in broad daylight. The neighbors grabbed their children and dogs and rushed inside. Starr waited for the sirens and the knock on the door, but they never came. No one called the police to report that a crime occurred. He had the man carried away in the back seat of a car.

Everything went as planned. She was done with Jose and his time was up, especially with her catching a case behind him. She had to speed up her plan. Usually, six to eight months was around the time that she would bleed men dry. By then they would trust her and let her into their world. Six months was enough in this case.

After cleaning his wounds and bandaging his head, she gave him two pain pills for a headache. She then attended to her own wounds. Her lip was split; her face was bruised and swollen. She cleaned her wounds and applied makeup where needed. To disguise her split lip, she applied a heavy layer of lipstick. She checked back to see if the pain pills had knocked Jose out. Once she noticed he was asleep, she removed all of her personal belongings from the house. Normally, she wouldn't have kept any more than an overnight bag at one of her target's homes. However, Jose spoiled her so much that he would buy her outfits and shoes on a whim. She practically had her own closet full of clothes at his house.

During that week, she had slowly taken things from the closet that she wanted to keep. Jose's taste in clothes was different from hers. Jose liked to buy her colorful outfits where the pattern just didn't matter to him. It could be dogs barking up and down the legs of a pair of pants and he would buy it for her. The times that she would be able to join him on a shopping spree; she purchased things she liked. She wouldn't be caught dead wearing half of the things he purchased on his own.

When she was done picking through the closet for some of the things she liked, she placed her bag outside the front door. She went back to check on Jose, who was still asleep. She could hear him snoring. She tiptoed back out of the room and placed the call.

"Hey, I'm ready. Give me five minutes before you send the car," she said and hung up.

Starr crept past the room and into the kitchen. She opened the cabinet under the sink where the water softener sat. She carefully removed it from under the sink. It wasn't connected. She quietly placed it on the floor then paused to make sure that she didn't hear any movement from the other room. She removed the cutout wood where the softener once sat. There she found the stacks of money he hid there. She removed each stack as fast as she could and placed them in a trash bag. When she was done, she placed the board back in place and the water softener. She placed the trash bag full of money outside with the rest of her things.

She went back into the room, where Jose was still sleeping. Quietly, she pulled out the table's drawer to retrieve a pen and paper.

She wrote; *I went to visit Aunt Pearl. I will be back soon. Love you.*

She kissed the paper, leaving a rouge-colored lip stain on the paper, and left it on the table. Looking over at Jose, she felt that she had made a mistake. He was a sleeping demon. He was a short man, but he was big. If things didn't go as planned, she knew her life would be in great danger. She did that many times. Never did she have to endure beatings in the process. She was tired of fighting with Jose. She was also facing charges behind her scheme. It had to come to an end.

The ball was already in motion and there was no way to stop it, even if she tried. Starr walked out the door and didn't look back. A car waited for her. She closed the door quietly behind her and picked up her bags. As she walked to the waiting car, she scanned the street for another vehicle. Before she stepped into the car, a black SUV with tinted windows moved slowly up the street towards Jose's home. There was no turning back. She felt something she hadn't felt before, nervousness.

Just like the others before him, he would go away for a very long time. He wouldn't suspect that she set him up, because her plan was flawless. Each hit was years apart. She would stick by each one of them by attending every court hearing, talking to the lawyer, putting money on his books, and visits. The key was to do some time with him until the big blow up. That part was usually easy. She would confront him about another woman on the outside or she would be seen in a questionable situation with another man, giving him something to fight with her about. She was sure he would find out, because word on the streets travels quicker to the jails. Then, voilà—it was over. She had a bad feeling about that one. She prayed that her vengeance for the things that happened to her as a child, would not be the death of her.

CHAPTER 17

After Starr was dropped off at home, she saw King's car in the driveway. She wasn't ready to face him just yet. Instead of taking her bags in the house, she placed them in her car and headed out to see Aunt Pearl. It had been a while since she saw her and she had to stick to her plan just in case.

Starr checked her rear view mirror several times on the way. Paranoia was something she wasn't familiar with. She'd run the scam before. It was like a walk in the park, but it just didn't seem right. She didn't love Jose, but she feared him. She saw the things that he and his friends did to torture others. Frustrated, she hit the steering wheel hard, honking the horn.

"Damn it!" she said. She struck the steering wheel again.

She thought about calling Jose's cell phone to see if he would answer. It was too soon to call. She needed confirmation that he was in police custody. No one knew, but King about the things that she did. He didn't approve of it and warned her that one day things would catch up to her if she didn't stop.

Starr pulled up to the four-story building that Aunt Pearl called home. They were designed as nice upscale apartments, with granite countertops, stainless steel appliances, and hardwood floors. It had been a few months since she'd last seen Aunt Pearl, and she dreaded the visit. There was something about Aunt Pearl where she could read her like a book. She knew that she loved her genuinely and cared about her well-being, but she couldn't help but feel judged at times. Her tell-like-it-is attitude didn't spare anyone's feelings. She didn't want to hear about the wrong she did. She wanted her to tell her how everything would be all right. There was always warning in their conversations, and she couldn't say that she was always wrong. There were times that she wished she had listened.

Starr knocked softly on the door of the apartment. She was fidgety, twirling her key chain in her hand.

"Who is it?" Aunt Pearl asked from behind the door.

"It's me, Starr," she said, in a jittery voice. She shifted nervously on her feet.

She could hear a chain being removed and a lock turn. She was anxious to get the visit over with.

The door opened quickly, and Aunt Pearl appeared scowling.

"You must be in some kind of trouble to just show up here without calling," she said with her brows drawn.

"Well, are you going to let me in?" she asked. She stopped shifting on her feet when a small smile softened Aunt Pearl's expression.

"You are always welcome, more than you know."

Starr ran for a hug and held her frail body tightly. She

swallowed hard as she tried to hide her emotions. The door closed hard behind her, breaking her from the embrace.

"I missed you so much. I was going to visit you sooner, but I've been busy."

Aunt Pearl looked into her eyes and she looked away. She pressed her small hand against Starr's cheek and shook her head.

"You never could apply makeup. I can see right through it," Aunt Pearl said. She walked away slowly with a slight limp.

Starr looked to the floor.

"How are you feeling?" Starr asked with concern.

"I'm just fine. Don't worry about me. What's going on with you?" She made it to her chair. She placed both hands on the arm and lowered herself slowly into the chair.

"Are you ready for your big Fourth of July cookout?"

"You know I am. I must be driving all of them crazy with my plans. It's not much that I can do from here."

Starr never saw Aunt Pearl move so slowly before. She appeared tired and winded from the walk from the door to her chair.

"Can I get you something from the kitchen?"

"A glass of water would be just fine."

Starr went into the kitchen. She opened the freezer and it was packed with food. She filled the glass with ice. She opened the refrigerator and found it full of food as well. She retrieved the jug of water and poured it into the glass.

"Are you eating?" she asked from the kitchen. She checked the cabinets and they were filled too. Every two weeks, she knew Michelle shopped for food for Aunt Pearl.

"I eat just fine, thank you," she responded gruffly.

Starr brought out the glass of water to Aunt Pearl.

Fighting the urge to sit at her feet and tell her all of her troubles; instead, she sat on the sofa.

"How come it looks like you haven't been eating? You have enough food in here to feed an army. Are you sure you're okay?"

"I pay for a meal plan here. When I don't feel like cooking, I go down and eat. Is that a problem?"

"No, not at all. I just want to make sure you're eating."

"It may not look like it, but I eat pretty well here. You know Loreal and Michelle come by twice a week and have dinner with me. They bring my grandbabies by here and we all just have a good time. King even comes when I ask him to."

"That's nice. I would come, but..."

"I don't want to hear no excuses from you. I raised you as my own, you and King. All I want is for you to stop doing whatever you out here doing. I don't see any good coming from all this trouble you in."

"Trouble? Who said I was in trouble?"

"I know you were just arrested. King told me all about it. Starr, you listen to me. Trouble is just that, trouble. You're playing with fire, baby girl, and you're about to burn the house down. Those games you're playing with these men are going to get you in something you ain't gon' be able to get out of. I warned you time and time again; bury that hate in your heart. What happened to you wasn't right, but you can't take it out on every man you meet."

Starr couldn't stop the tears from falling. The truth and the warning she couldn't ignore. It was confirmed; she fucked up.

"I don't know what to do. I messed up this time."

Aunt Pearl held her arms out to Starr. "Come here,

baby." Starr melted into her arms, sobbing. "You need to ask for forgiveness, and then you need to forgive. Let it go, child. Let it go."

"I don't know how to let it go. Every day I hurt, knowing I will never have children. He took that away from me. He took my babies! No man wants a rotten woman!"

Aunt Pearl lifted Starr's face by her chin and looked her directly in her eyes.

"You are special. God saw fit to breathe life into you, child. He never left you. You have to let it go and live life without all that anger." Aunt Pearl took a deep breath and held Starr's face tight to her chest. She allowed her to weep. Starr wept deeply, crying out in long screams for minutes. Aunt Pearl held her until she was all cried out.

"I love you, Aunt Pearl." Starr kissed her cheek.

"I love you too, Starlene."

"Aunt Pearl, you know I don't like when you call me that," Starr said with a small laugh. She used her hands to wipe her tears.

"I know. I just wanted to see that pretty smile."

Knock! Knock!

"Are you expecting someone?" Starr asked. She walked to the door.

"No, not that I know of. Today has been full of surprises."

Without asking whom it was or looking out of the peephole, she opened the door. There stood Jose with his head still bandaged.

Jose walked in, looking behind him as if he was being followed. Starr backed away from the door slowly, as Jose stepped behind the door and closed it. He continued to look out into the hallway.

"What are you doing here? I told you I would be back later," Starr said nervously. She was afraid for herself and

Aunt Pearl. Jose wasn't supposed to be there. He was supposed to be in lock up and possibly on the next thing smoking back to Mexico.

"My house was raided. I was in a shootout with police," Jose said breathlessly.

"What? How did you get away?"

"I shot my way out. I killed one of them, too."

"Oh, my God! Why did you come here? This is my aunt's place. Why did you bring this here?"

"Why are you acting like that? You should be glad your man got away!"

"I am, but you shouldn't have come here. What if you were followed?"

"I'm here now. I need to tell you something."

"What?"

"I'm going back to Mexico and I want you to come with me. I can't stay here with all this heat. They are going to fry me for killing that cop."

"I can't go with you to Mexico."

"Why not? You are my lady."

Starr didn't know what to say and shifted on her feet. That wasn't part of the plan. Her words came slower as her mind raced. *He said he killed a cop.* She prayed it wasn't Agent Mosley. She and Agent Mosley had a special arrangement. He took the credit for collaring Richmond's most wanted kingpins. He was the officer who saved her life; he was the first officer on the scene when she was found in the alley. At that time, he was a rookie and had only been on the force for eighteen months. He visited her every day during her hospitalization and kept in touch with her ever since. He had since become a federal agent and she was glad she'd found a way to repay him for saving her life.

"Starr, who is it baby?" Aunt Pearl called out.

Starr turned her head in the direction of Aunt Pearl's voice. "I can't leave my aunt. She is not doing well at all. If I leave her, I'm afraid she will die and I won't be here. Please, don't ask me to choose. After all that she's done for me, the least I can do is be here for her. You understand that, don't you?" she asked nervously.

Jose peered down on her as his eyes narrowed. His jaw tightened and his head tilted. Starr took a step back.

"And, who is this handsome fellow?" Aunt Pearl said, startling them both.

Starr was relieved to see Aunt Pearl walking toward them. "Auntie, this is Jose," Starr said.

"Hi," Jose said. His demeanor slowly softened.

"Hi," Aunt Pearl said dryly. She eyed them both suspiciously.

"Jose was just leaving. I'll be back in a minute."

"Hurry up and come back. We need to finish our conversation."

"Yes, ma'am," Starr said.

"Let's talk out here," Starr said. She walked past Jose, brushing against him to open the door. He followed behind her.

"I'm leaving now. Are you coming?" Jose asked.

"No, I can't. I love you, Jose, but right now is not a good time. Maybe I can visit for now, until I'm able to stay permanently." She reached for him and he stepped back from her. She grabbed him and pulled him close to her. She kissed him passionately. "I love you, Jose, and you know that. I just can't go with you right now," she said.

"Okay, I have to get out of here. I will contact you as soon as I can."

She walked him to the elevators. As they waited for the elevator to return, they hugged and kissed. Starr's heart pounded in her chest, but she held it together. The elevator arrived and the doors slowly opened while they were embraced.

"Put your hands up!" a voice shouted from the elevator. Three guns were pointed at them.

Starr jumped back with her hands in the air, but Jose didn't move.

"I said put your fucking hands up!" a man said.

Jose slowly lifted his hands in the air. Three agents exited the elevator, and one of them arrested Jose. Another agent put Starr against the wall and placed handcuffs on her.

"Leave her out of this. She has nothing to do with this," Jose said. "Get those damn cuffs off her!"

"Shut up, big boy!" the agent said.

"Fuck you!" Jose shouted. He spat at the agent.

The agent quickly rushed Jose into the elevator with the other agent. He slammed Jose against the elevator wall face first. Jose spat blood from his mouth onto the floor.

Starr was still pinned against the wall with her hands cuffed behind her back.

"Jose!" she screamed, as the elevator doors closed.

When the doors closed and the elevator descended down, the agent turned her around to face him.

"Good job, little lady," the agent said. He removed the handcuffs.

"What?" she asked confused, as she rubbed her wrists.

"Agent Mosley told us where you could be found, in case something went wrong."

"Is Agent Mosley okay?"

"He's in surgery. He was shot, but he will survive."

"Thank you, Jesus! Tell him I will see him soon and that I'm sorry."

The agent nodded as he walked to the elevators.

Starr walked back to Aunt Pearl's with a smile on her face. She breathed a sigh of relief. Jose was finally gone.

CHAPTER 18

It was Fourth of July weekend and Aunt Pearl hosted her annual Independence Day cookout. She made sure she came home to continue her tradition. The backyard was filled with family, friends, and neighbors. Everyone looked forward to her annual cookouts. For two days, she prepped and marinated everything she could think of in advance.

King manned the grills under Aunt Pearl's close supervision. He went inside to call Starr for the third time, but he didn't answer any of his calls. Aunt Pearl asked several times where she was. As usual, she disappointed Aunt Pearl by not showing up for family gatherings or visits to see her.

"Hey, Cousin," Loreal said. She walked in the house with an armful of bags. King took the bags from her and placed them in the kitchen.

"What's up?" he asked. "Where is Robert?"

"He'll be here later. He started working on the leak under the kitchen sink and managed to break something. Could you believe that?" she said jokingly.

"Robert needs to call a handyman sometimes. The last time I came over, he almost blew the house up, messing around with the wiring."

"I don't know what to do with him sometimes. How has the pregnancy been going?"

"So, far so good."

The screened door slammed shut. Both King and Loreal looked to the door. Maya, seven months pregnant, wobbled in with a tray of barbecue ribs hot off the grill.

"Hey, Maya!" Loreal said.

King rushed over to relieve her of the large pan of food. He kissed her on the cheek and smiled at her.

"Loreal! I was waiting for you and Michelle. I wanted to show you what we've done to the baby's room. Oh, and thanks for the bedding. It goes perfectly with the baby's theme."

"Michelle should be here in a minute. Why don't you sit down? You don't need to be on your feet too much."

Loreal and Maya sat down at the table in conversation. King loved to see Maya and his family getting along so well. Some of his friends weren't fortunate enough to have that kind of peace.

"King, can you give Maya some water? It's too hot out there for her and the baby," Loreal asked.

He gave them both bottled water and went outside to help Aunt Pearl.

It was sweltering outside. The heat immediately engulfed him but the sweltering heat didn't faze Aunt Pearl. She was on the grills, flipping burgers on one and steaks on another.

"King, there you are. I sent Maya inside, because it's too hot out here right now for her," Aunt Pearl said.

King wrapped his arms around her and kissed her

cheek. That was the only way to get the two grilling utensils out of her hands without a fight.

"I love you, too, now get off me. It's too hot for all that," she said.

King was successful in taking over the grilling duties. Aunt Pearl went inside to cool off. He looked up to find Richie in attendance.

"What's up?" Richie called out.

"What's good, man?" King said.

They embraced each other in a brotherly hug. He hadn't seen Richie for three months. He was locked up for driving on a suspended license.

"You got out just in time for Aunt Pearl's barbecue, huh?" King said.

"Yeah, I timed it just right, didn't I?" Richie asked.

The young woman standing behind Richie, rudely cleared her throat. Richie rolled his eyes in her direction and took a deep breath.

"This is my friend, Sheneeta," Richie said.

"What's up, Sheneeta? I'm King."

"I know who you are. Don't you remember me from high school? Didn't you go out with a girl named Maya?"

King pretended to take a closer look at her. He recognized her, but didn't want to make it obvious.

"Yeah, Maya is my wife."

"Wife? No, you didn't wife her. She thought she was all that in school," Sheneeta said.

"That's high school shit. Don't be so disrespectful," Richie said.

"What did I do? He know she's a bourgeois bitch, too!"

"Yo, Richie, get this bitch out of here. Disrespectful ass," King said.

Richie grabbed Sheneeta by the arm and yelled at her.

The guests stopped what they were doing and focused on the drama.

"I can't take your ghetto ass nowhere! You're always running your damn mouth. Shut the fuck up sometimes!" Richie said, pulling her towards the gate.

"Richie, who is that?" Aunt Pearl asked. She, Maya, Michelle, and Loreal walked out to the deck.

"Oh, shit," King said under his breath.

"Nobody, Aunt Pearl. She was just leaving," Richie said, still holding Sheneeta by the arm.

"Sheneeta?" asked Maya.

"Oh, now you know my name. You were too good to speak in school, so don't speak to me now!" Sheneeta shouted, as she struggled to free her arm from Richie's grip.

"Where did you find this one at? You sure know how to pick them," Michelle said sarcastically.

"I don't know who you think you're talking about. You don't know me. Forget all y'all," Sheneeta screamed out. "And, you get your damn hands off me. I can find my own way out. I didn't want to come, anyway."

Richie let go of her arm and opened the gate for her. She eyed him and walked out. She turned and gave him the finger.

"Let's keep this party going. Hey DJ, play the "Electric Slide" for me," Aunt Pearl said.

The mood quickly changed as people lined up for the line dance. Maya and King even joined in. As usual, Aunt Pearl's celebration was full of excitement and good eating.

CHAPTER 19

It was midnight. The humid night air mixed with aromas from nearby restaurants flowed through a raised window of Starr's third-floor condo. She'd moved into the condo two weeks prior without telling anyone, not even King. The air conditioning unit needed service. Boxes were still stacked against the freshly painted, soft tan walls.

She wanted a fresh start in life without her past chasing her. After her last set up, Jose, she knew it wouldn't be long before her luck would run out. It was time for her to finally find love and experience a real relationship, a relationship with no motives. She was sitting pretty with all the money she stole from her victims. Jose was the biggest come up. He kept one hundred-thousand in the house at all times.

Starr tossed and turned in her queen-sized bed. Sweat formed on her body, making her white tank top cling to her. Her heart slammed around in her chest as she watched herself in a recurring dream. She watched her younger self from above lying on her back in what appeared to be a half-paved and graveled alley. The fenced in backyards of homes and garages lined both sides of the alley. A City of Richmond green dumpster was beside her. A faceless man stood over her younger self, as she lay there dazed, staring up at him.

"No, please, stop," she moaned in her sleep. She kicked the blanket off.

In her dream, she saw the faceless man draw a shiny knife and raise it above her body. Her younger self didn't move, didn't speak, and didn't fight. With all of her might, she tried to pull herself down toward her younger self, but fought against gravity. She willed herself to come out of the hovering state her body was in, but nothing happened. She fought harder as she called out to her younger self, "Fight!" It was too late. The knife came down toward her younger self in slow motion. Starr clutched her stomach as she felt the cold, sharp slice of the knife to her abdomen.

RING!

Her cell phone rang loudly and vibrated at the same time. She sat up quickly, breathing heavily and exhausted from the struggle in her sleep. The phone rang loudly a second time followed by a vibration. She looked down at her stomach. She lifted her tank top and touched the scar that interrupted her tight abs and extended from above her navel down to her pelvic area. A third ring snapped her back to reality.

"Hello?" she answered.

"What's up?" King asked.

"Hey, is everything okay? It's late."

A short moment of silence fell between them. Starr began to feel uncomfortable.

"Where were you today? You know Aunt Pearl is upset that you didn't show up for the cookout."

"I was busy. By the time I finished, it was too late to come by. How was it, anyway?"

"Why do you make shit so hard? All she asked is for you to show your face sometimes. You always talking about how you don't have a family, but you push the only family you have away. All you're worried about is the next lick."

Her stomach rose from his hurtful words.

"Excuse me? The last I checked, you were just as fucked up as I am. Don't try to throw my past in my face. I'm trying to change; I'm working on me. If you don't support what I'm trying to do, then you can fuck off with the rest of them!"

"I can't keep worrying about you all the time. When one of those gangsters you dealing with fuck you up once he figures out what you're all about, don't call me. If you say, you're trying to change, then good for you. I have a child and a wife to worry about now."

"You never had to worry about me, because I got this. Yes, I am changing for the better. Jose was my last lick. I even have my own place now. Just so, you know; I met somebody that I really like this time. No games."

"That's good to hear, Starr. How do you expect us to know what's going on with you, if you don't even come over or call to let us know? Especially me, I'm your brother!"

"You're tripping. Just call me tomorrow when you calm down, before we say something we both will regret."

There was a moment of silence.

"Where are you staying?" King took in a deep breath.

"You'll know soon enough. I'm planning on inviting everyone over for dinner soon."

"See, there you go again. I can't know where you live?"

"No, it's not like that. I just want to have my place straight first. I know as soon as you get the address, you're going to be on the first thing smoking."

"A'ight then. Call me tomorrow and text me your address."

"I will. Love you, little brother."

"Yeah right. I'm still mad at your ass."

"Whatever! Bye, boy!"

She and King still found themselves fighting from time to time. It wasn't that she didn't want to be around the family, but she'd been feeling paranoid ever since the incident with Jose. She'd been looking over her shoulders more than usual. She never wanted to bring harm to her family, which was why she decided to move out and change her life.

She reached over her bed for the plastic red cup and bottle of vodka that sat on an unpacked box. She poured herself a cup of warm vodka and sipped. A loud motorcycle sped down the street and stopped in front of her building. She walked over to the window and looked down to the street. There was a blue and black motorcycle in front of her building. She watched a man park his motorcycle and walk into her building.

Starr hurriedly downed as much of her drink as she could without choking. She rushed out into the living room to gather Chinese food boxes, empty soda cans, and dirty paper plates. She grabbed as much of the trash as she could, quickly walked into the kitchen, and dropped the armful of trash into the trash can.

The house phone rang.

"Hello?" she answered.

"Tone is here to see you. Should I let him up?" the security guard asked.

"Yes. Please send him up, thanks."

Starr quickly let down her ponytail and ran her fingers through her hair. She tucked the left side behind her ear. She raced into her master bathroom to retrieve her makeup bag. She rummaged through to find a sheer pink gloss. She applied the gloss to her lips and gave herself a last once-over in the mirror. She combed through her hair.

Starr opened the front door, just as the elevator arrived on the third floor.

"Hey, you. You're early," Starr said. She gave Tone a hug and walked back to her apartment.

"What's wrong with me being early? You knew I was coming," he said. He stopped short at the door.

Starr turned toward him. Tone had a serious look on his face.

"What's wrong?" she asked.

"Did you have somebody else over here?"

"No, I didn't. I just didn't expect you here so soon."

Tone walked into the apartment slowly. Starr closed and locked the door behind him. He sat his helmet down on the table and took a seat on the sofa. She sat down beside him.

"I'm sorry. I didn't mean to accuse you of anything," he said apologetically.

Starr became annoyed with his constant accusations of her cheating. She knew that he would be apologetic for the remainder of the night as he always did. His reason behind his mistrust was the fact that his ex-girlfriend cheated on him with one of his friends. He had a hard time trusting females after that.

"You have to stop being so insecure if you want this to work. There isn't anyone else in my life right now, except you. I have no reason to lie to you," she explained.

"I believe you. I promise this is the last time. I love you and I know I can trust you," he said. He kissed her gently, parting her lips with his tongue. They shared a heavy kiss.

Starr was quickly reminded why she put up with his insecurities. He made love to her like no other. He was the best where it all counted. His tongue traced hers as his hands palmed her breast. She moaned as he tongued her down. He gently pushed her back onto the sofa; she didn't resist and let him have his way with her.

CHAPTER 20

It was after midnight as King listened at the bedroom door to be sure that Maya was still snoring. King looked up a phone number in his smartphone, and then placed it back in his pocket. He pulled out another cell phone, this one, a basic flip phone. He dialed the number and pressed send.

"I'm at the spot," Gooch said, without greeting him.

"I'm on my way," King said. He placed the cell phone back in his pocket and entered his bedroom.

Maya laid on her side with her beautifully rounded belly covered in pink zebra-print pajamas. Her hair was tied up with a scarf. He pulled the blanket over her. Ever since he had a central air conditioning system installed, the house was always freezing. A far cry from when he was growing up with fans placed in windows, circulating hot air around the house. He sat on the edge of the bed next to her, and admired her smooth dark skin. Running his hands down the side of her face, he aroused her from her sleep.

"What are you still doing up?" she asked. She tried to turn over on her back, but not without some difficulty. With King's assistance, she turned on her back. He kissed and rubbed her belly, something he couldn't resist doing when her belly was exposed.

"It's Richie. He needs a ride. I don't want him getting in any trouble driving without a license," he lied. He knew she could usually tell when he was lying to her, because he would avoid making eye contact with her. Instead, he fumbled with his shoelaces as he spoke to her.

"Okay, baby. Be careful," she said. She sat up, kissed him on the cheek and turned back over to sleep.

King didn't like lying to her, but he couldn't tell her where he was really going. Maya would never understand why this was so important to him. He could see her trying to talk him out of it and holding him hostage, so that he couldn't leave. He kissed her, and then her belly before leaving.

On the drive to meet Gooch, his stomach flipped and turned. He wasn't sure what to expect. Gooch had given him strict instructions on where he should be, which side of the street to park on, and exactly what he should be paying close attention to.

King followed his instructions exactly. He arrived at the spot at exactly one o'clock. He sat in the parking lot of the store situated across from a house known for its traffic of unsavory individuals. The house sat on a corner, with three houses to the left of it.

The house was dark and there didn't seem to be any movement inside. King went inside the store to purchase a drink and chips. On the way back to his car, he saw a young woman exit the house and cross the street to where he was. She appeared to be about sixteen years old. She was dressed in cutoff shorts, with the pockets hanging down below the shorts, and a red fitted shirt. White earplugs dangled from her ears to her pockets and she bopped her head to whatever she was listening to. King wondered if she lived at the house and if her parents knew she was out at that time of morning.

He stepped back into his car and opened his drink as he watched her enter the store. It was time. He looked toward the house, paying close attention to the side street. Gooch appeared either drunk or high. He staggered and swayed as he walked up the side street slowly, stopping midway. Then, two men exited the front door of the house, standing on the front porch. One of the men was tall and the other was short. The two men faced the main street and paid no attention to the side street. The tall one walked down the steps toward the street as the other turned to go back into the house. As soon as the man walked down the sidewalk in the opposite direction of Gooch, King saw in his peripheral the young girl leaving the store.

"Shit," he said under his breath. His adrenaline pumped faster as he anticipated witnessing a murder and possibly one of a young girl. Gooch seemed to sober quickly as his pace sped up and he was a few paces behind the man. King looked back and forth from Gooch to the young girl.

Gooch moved in quickly behind the man and fired a bullet into the back of his head. If it weren't for the loud popping sound, it would've been hard to determine what made the man fall to the ground. The corner streetlight was out and the only light was the store sign. The man dropped face down on the sidewalk. The young girl screamed and ran back towards the store. He watched as

Gooch fired several more shots into the man's body. Gooch ran back in the direction he came in.

Moments later, the man who was on the porch ran out of the house. He walked down the steps slowly with a pistol in hand, looking in all directions. He walked out to the sidewalk, frantically looking back scanning the area. When he caught sight of his friend, he ran over, knelt down and ran through his pockets. He placed what he found in his own pockets. When he was done, he placed the pistol in his back, stood to his feet and placed a call. He paced back and forth near the body.

At the first sign of sirens, King pulled out of the parking lot with his adrenaline still pumping. Gooch instructed him not to make any phone calls while in the area. King thought about how easy Gooch made the murder look. He didn't seem to hesitate for one second. He was in control of the situation. King took mental notes and hoped that he had the nerve to actually go through with it when the time came. He realized that pulling a trigger wasn't as easy as it seemed, especially for a virgin like himself. Gooch was right; he had to get his hands dirty.

~~~

Two weeks later, King met Gooch at Richie's house. Richie didn't want to be in the middle of King's vengeance, but he supported him. Richie still lived in K.C. with his mother and was a ladies man. He had three baby mothers and five children.

"What's up, bruh?" Richie said, giving King a manly hug.

"Ain't nothing. What's up with you?" King asked.

"Same ole, same ole. So, you are really serious about this shit?" Richie said.

"You know better than anybody about that shit. You were there with me. We both had nightmares behind that. Before I hit the dirt, I'm going to kill him. I went to the police station to get information on her case. I know it was somebody from around here," King said.

"I just don't think your mom would've wanted you to fuck your life up, and end up in prison for the rest of your life. Just let Gooch handle that shit," Richie said.

Gooch entered the room, scratching his arm viciously. When he saw King, he smiled.

"My protégé, King," he said, as he pounded on his chest. He stopped in the doorway of the living room.

"What's up, Gooch?" King said. He could tell that Gooch was high. It was said he was most dangerous when he was high. That was something that didn't make sense to King. He thought that a clear head would be a better state of mind to be in.

"We have a job tonight. Two for the price of one," Gooch said.

King, Richie, and Gooch rode in the car that Gooch showed up in. The ride was quiet, other than Gooch giving Richie directions. They pulled into a subdivision with beautiful homes. Even in the dark, there was curb appeal. They came to a home with few lights. It appeared as if no one was home. The porch light wasn't on and a car was in the driveway. They drove by the house slowly at Gooch's command. Through the front window, two people could be seen sitting at a table across from each other.

"Turn around up here and park across the street," Gooch said.

Richie followed Gooch's orders and parked in front of an empty lot, across from the home that Gooch pointed out. The house was in an upscale part of town in a new subdivision where there were still empty lots for sale. Richie cut off the lights and the car. There was a moment of silence. King was in the back seat, nervous. He didn't know where they were and what would happen. He was too scared to ask any questions, so he waited patiently for Gooch to speak.

Finally, Gooch spoke, "King, it's time. I have two targets in that house. I am willing to let you have one," Gooch said.

King's stomach rumbled. He wasn't mentally prepared for this; he thought hard about what he asked of him.

"Who is the target?" King asked.

"It don't matter. Do you want one or not? If you think you're going to pop your cherry on the invisible man, you are sadly mistaken. You think it's going to be easy to find the man that killed your mom and pull that trigger? It's not. You have to have ice in your veins to do this shit and you don't," Gooch said.

"What do you want me to do?" King asked nervously.

"Aim and shoot," Gooch said. Gooch handed him a pair of black gloves. He pulled them on and then he handed him a gun.

King reluctantly reached for the gun. "Rich, let me get that bandana," he asked.

Richie reached in his back pocket and handed King the folded bandana. He tied the bandana over the bottom half of his face, where he could still see. Before he could finish, Gooch exited the car. He opened the door and stepped out too. Gooch was already on the other side of the street. By the time he caught up to Gooch, he'd already kicked in the front door.

"Stay low and close," Gooch whispered. Gooch scaled

the wall, with his gun leading the way. King moved close behind him with his head low.

The lights went out in a nearby room, rendering them blind. King blinked a few times to adjust to the darkness. A shadow moved quickly down the hall from them and gunfire rang out. Gooch returned fire and advanced further into the house, leaving a petrified King behind.

King was scared. He took a deep breath and let the gun lead the way. He quickly looked down the hall to make sure no one would fire at him. He wanted to get closer to where he could duck into a room. He saw Gooch in the hallway; Gooch motioned for King to come closer, and he moved in nervously. He knew that he heard two different guns; someone fired back. A bullet flew past him, landing in the wall behind him. Gooch didn't flinch. A dark shadow emerged into the hallway and Gooch took him out with one shot. Gooch walked closer to the body on the floor, and fired two more shots.

King was three feet behind Gooch near an entranceway. Gooch motioned for him to enter the room on his left. Gunfire erupted, sending Gooch down to his knees as bullets sprayed the wall behind him. King crept slowly through the living room, scaling the wall. He saw a man shooting from the kitchen with his back to him. He didn't look in his direction, because he watched Gooch.

King had the shot. His heart raced and he could feel his adrenaline rushing through his body.

It was now or never, he thought.

He had to make a move before he was spotted. He was wide open. He pointed the gun and fired at the man. The bullet entered through the back of the man's head, sending him against the wall and sliding onto the floor.

"Clear!" Gooch shouted.

King was still standing with the gun pointed at the man's dead body, trembling. Blood and matter covered the wall behind the body. The sight sent him into a panic attack. He couldn't breathe as he stared at the blood. His vision flashed, his body went numb, and he began to hyperventilate.

"We have to go!" Gooch shouted.

King didn't move, because he had tunnel vision. He saw flashes of his mother's bloody bedroom and the blood trail that was left. He shook with the gun still in hand. Gooch dragged King out of the house and to the car. He didn't say a word.

"What the hell is wrong with him?" Richie asked, looking in the back seat at King. He drove recklessly out of the neighborhood. King was in a fetal position in the back seat, knees pulled tight to his chest.

"He'll be fine. He got what he wanted," Gooch said.

"He did it?" Richie asked.

"He blew his brains out with one shot. Then, he went in shock. That's what happens the first time," Gooch said.

King could hear Richie and Gooch's conversation. He was conflicted. He'd killed somebody for practice. He was more affected by his own response to the sight of blood. He thought he was over those episodes, but it was clear he was still affected by it. After ten minutes of being lost in thought, he pushed through the wall. He sat up and rolled down the window for fresh air. No one said a word as they drove back to Richie's house.

CHAPTER 21

Starr and Tone had been dating for four months, and she found herself falling in love for the very first time. She'd been with other men that satisfied her in one way or the other, but Tone was different. He was kind, handsome, giving, well endowed, and skilled in the bedroom. He came at the perfect time in her life, right when she decided to stop ruining men's lives and pursue happiness. She began to reinvent herself.

Starr rolled over in her bed and rested her head on Tone's chest as he slept. She listened to his lungs fill with air and to his strong heartbeat. She smiled as she played with his few chest hairs. The thought of waking up in his arms every morning warmed her heart.

"Good morning," he said. He yawned and stretched.

"Good morning to you," she said with a smile. "Are you hungry? I was about to make breakfast."

He eyed her seductively as his soldier stood at attention. She was still naked. He watched her throw on his shirt that was too big for her.

"Don't look at me like that. Didn't you get enough last night?" She teased him by bending over, exposing her naked butt.

"I can go for some right now," he said.

Starr turned around to find him stroking himself openly. She wanted him. A hard one always turned her on. Still bare from the waist down, she walked over to Tone's side of the bed. She straddled him and lowered herself slowly onto him. Her tightness slowly parted for his girth.

"Shit," he moaned. He pushed inside her hard, sending waves of pleasure up her spine. She matched his intensity by slamming down hard onto him. She pressed downward, forcing him deeper inside. She pulled herself up and down, tightening every muscle in her midsection.

"I'm about to..." Tone moaned. He pulled Starr closer to him, plunging one of her breasts into his mouth. He sucked hard.

"Me too," she moaned.

With that said, Tone grabbed her butt and began to lift her faster and harder on him. After they both had reached their peak together, Starr collapsed on top of him.

"Damn, that was good. Now I'm starving." Tone said, smacking her on the butt.

Starr jumped off him from the sting of his slap and rubbed out the sting.

"That's what I was trying to do before you made me come back and put it on you again," she said.

Starr cooked breakfast and they both ate. After breakfast, Tone cleaned the kitchen against Starr's wishes. While he cleaned the kitchen, Starr took a shower. When Tone was done, he decided to join her in the shower. He went into her bedroom to join her in the master bath. He opened the door to the bathroom when her cell phone rang. He continued into the bathroom, but decided to see who was calling. He quietly shut the door and walked over to the bed where she left her cell phone. A picture of a teenage Starr and a young boy was on the screen. He answered the phone.

"Hello?" Tone answered, in a deep, but stern voice.

"Hello?" King asked.

"Who is this?" Tone asked. He didn't care who was on the other end, but he wanted to let them know he was the man in her life with just those three words.

"Who is this? Where is Starr?" King asked. Tone could hear the frustration in the caller's voice. That was just the reaction he wanted.

"She can't come to the phone right now. She's in the shower," Tone said slyly.

"Tell her to call her brother," King said, before hanging up.

Tone looked at the phone and gave a short laugh. He looked closer at the phone and thought that the boy's face was one he recognized from his past. His heart skipped a beat and he forgot to breathe. A second later, the screen went black and the picture was gone. He dropped her phone back on the bed then dropped to the bed and fell back, grabbing his head in disbelief.

~~~

King was in the waiting room of the doctor's office with Maya. She was scheduling the following week's appointment. The pregnancy moved along well. Maya's glow and beautiful round belly always put a smile on his face. It gave him a sense of pride to love and be with the woman that carried his first child. She was giving him

SNOOK

something he never had. A child of his own that would have his last name. He always felt alone in the world, no parents, brothers, or sisters. He was soon to be blessed with a child of his own.

"Who were you talking to like that?" Maya asked. She'd heard the short conversation and noticed the frustration on his face.

"I called Starr and this clown answered the phone, trying to be a badass," he explained.

"I didn't know she was dating again! After Jose was deported, she seemed so hurt. Well, I guess she moved on. That could be a good thing," she said.

The nurse handed her an appointment card and she thanked her. They left the doctor's office. On the way to the elevator, King's phone rang and he looked at Maya. She didn't like when he took personal calls when they were spending time together. After the appointment, they were going out to lunch and a movie.

"Go ahead. Answer it," she said. She pressed the down button on the elevator.

He looked at his phone to see who the caller was. "It's Starr," he said, ignoring the call.

"Why didn't you answer it? It could be important," Maya said.

"I'll talk to her later. She's up to her same old shit. These dudes just don't know what's up with her," he said.

The empty elevator arrived and the two of them stepped on. King pressed the button for the first floor. He pulled Maya close to him and held her.

"Why does it seem like all the dudes she gets involved with, end up locked up? What about the one that was shot during that robbery? I thought she was wrong for breaking up with him after he was paralyzed. Who does that?"

"Starr does. There's a lot about her you just don't know. Let's just leave it at that."

They stepped off the elevator into the lobby. On the way out the door to the parking lot, a couple was coming in. A man much taller than King bumped him hard, sending King back a step. Both Maya and the other young lady both stopped. King recognized him from the streets. He knew him by Roland. He had some weight in the streets and was known for his hands.

"Damn. What was that?" King asked. He was still holding the door for Maya. She stepped out onto the sidewalk.

"What the fuck you gon' do?" Roland asked. King stepped to the man. They were now face-to-face.

"No! Let's go. This is not worth it," Maya said.

"Yeah, it ain't worth you getting your ass kicked in front of your baby mama," Roland said.

The security guard heard the altercation and intervened. "What is going on out here?" the security officer asked. "Break it up and leave the premises, if you don't have business in this building."

"Come on, baby. Leave him alone. I'm about to be late for this appointment," the girl said.

Maya and King looked over at the girl; it was Sheneeta, with a baby bump. She'd come with Richie to Aunt Pearl's cookout. She'd dyed her hair blonde and cut it in a short bob.

"Sheneeta?" Maya asked.

"Yeah, it's me. You better get your man before he get his ass kicked," Sheneeta said.

"Last warning, fellows," the security guard said.

Sheneeta pulled Roland by the arm into the building. He allowed her to pull him as he gave King a cocky smirk.

"Let's go," Maya said.

King was ready to kill. His blood raced through his veins as he saw himself blowing the back of Roland's head off.

He walked to the car in almost a jog, leaving Maya wobbling behind. He unlocked the door, reached under the driver's seat, pulled out a pistol and slammed the car door.

"What are you doing? Where did you get that gun?" Maya cried out. King tried to push past Maya as she blocked him from leaving. "Are you going to knock me over with your baby just to get to him? You're going to be a father, you can't do this," she cried.

King couldn't hear what she was saying. His eyes were wild and he wanted blood for Roland's disrespect. "Move out of the way!" he shouted at her.

"No, you're not going to do something stupid and ruin our lives! Your daughter is going to grow up without a father, because you couldn't control yourself," she cried.

"Shit!" he shouted. "A'ight."

"Get in the car, King. We're going to end up running late for our movie, if we do not get to this restaurant," she said. She tried to lighten the situation by changing the subject.

Maya walked around to the passenger side of the car once she thought it was safe to do so. She opened the door and sat in the car. King stood outside the car for a few more minutes, just in case Roland came back out. When Roland didn't emerge from the office building, he drove away with his wife to their next destination without spilling blood.

CHAPTER 22

On the drive, both Maya and King sat quietly. He drove aggressively during the short distance to the diner. He had no mercy on the cobblestoned streets or his car. A switch was turned on and he couldn't turn it off. All of the anger he harbored in his soul danced around him, taunting him to act on his raw emotions.

"Are you okay?" Maya asked.

They came to a stoplight and he was finally forced to stop. He stepped on the brake hard, forcing Maya forward in her seat.

"I know you're mad, but you're not going to kill me in this car. Calm down!"

King didn't respond to her. He was at the stoplight, staring at it as if he dared it to turn green. After giving him a moment to respond, she sucked her teeth, then turned and faced the window.

He found parking in the lot beside the diner. Turning off the ignition, he took in a deep breath. It felt like he was deprived of oxygen and that one breath took him down a little. He took in another and gathered his thoughts. He knew that if he didn't calm down, he would hurt someone. That demon wasn't going to show itself in front of Maya.

"I'm sorry," he said.

Maya didn't answer as she reached in the back seat for her handbag.

"I said that I'm sorry. I don't know what you expected me to do. I'm a man and I'm not going to let another man carry me," he said.

"I know that, King. I just don't want anything to happen to you. I heard about him before. He's bad news," she said.

"Just forget about what happened and let's get some lunch."

"I didn't know you had a gun in the car. Is there something you need to tell me? You're not in any beef are you? I know Richie is still wild and he better not get you caught up in his mess."

"I'm good, now come on."

"Okay," she said reluctantly.

King needed the argument to end, because he already knew he couldn't win. He was well aware of Roland's reputation. He was from a rival housing project. His name was rumored in murder cases.

After lunch, Maya was tired and wanted to head home instead of the movies. That was fine with King, because he was in no mood to sit through a movie. She laid down for a nap as soon as they returned home.

King then called Richie.

"What's up?" Richie answered.

"Guess what the fuck happened today? I saw Sheneeta and Roland at the doctor's office together," King said.

"Hold up! She said she wasn't fucking with him like that. You know, she's trying to say I'm her baby daddy."

"I'm coming out the door; he bumped into me and started talking shit."

"Fuck him! He don't want no parts of K.C. We just got to beefing behind Sheneeta's ass. She called me around her house and she was outside with him. He talked a lot of shit, so I had to show him something."

"I was about to kill his ass. I went to the car to get my gun and Maya stopped me. If it wasn't for her, I know I would've killed him."

"What do you want to do? Just say the word."

King paused for a moment as he thought about what could've happened earlier. To hear that Richie also had a problem with Roland was alarming. He then understood. It wasn't personal. It was behind Richie. He saw them together on numerous occasions.

"Oh, I see now. He was mad at your ass," King said.

"I'd be mad as hell too after I got my ass whooped. Yo, let me hit you back," Richie said. He ended the call without waiting for King's response.

King retreated to the basement. The basement became his private man cave after Aunt Pearl moved out. The basement was finished and only needed a few things to make it his. He purchased a television, refrigerator and moved an old sofa into the basement. On the other side of the room was gym equipment. A weight bench, treadmill, and free weights lined the wall. A punching bag hung from the ceiling hoist.

That was where he went to fight his demons. No one was allowed in the basement without his consent, because there were things there that he didn't want anyone to ever see. He hid his demons from everyone, fighting the urge to kill anyone he thought would have had anything to do with his mother's death. That anger ate at his soul.

King took off his shirt, dropping it on the floor, as he quickly walked to the punching bag. His anger stirred inside. He circled the punching bag, never taking his eyes off it. Then, he unleashed his fists on the bag. He punched ferociously, spitting curse words between punches. That lasted until his arms became tired and he missed more punches than he connected. Falling against the bag, as sweat dripped down his body, he fought the tightness in his chest. He breathed heavily as he tried to catch his breath.

Completely exhausted, he stumbled over to the black mini fridge and retrieved a cold bottle of spring water. He twisted off the cap and gulped down the water. Using the back of his hand, he wiped away the cold water that dripped down his chin. He let the rest fall down onto his chest, cooling him down.

King found himself on middle ground once again. It seemed that it was harder and harder to control his rage. Running on the treadmill for fifteen minutes or lifting weights used to be enough to calm him. At that moment, he'd found himself beating a punching bag until it felt as if his heart would explode.

The next phase of his ritual was to check his boyhood journal he kept. He would read the names of possible suspects in his mother's death. At times, he would add and take away names as he pondered on those memories. The book was in a small locked file cabinet. No one had a key, except him. It was tucked behind his old, alphabetized comics in the second drawer. No one knew about the journal and the notes that he kept back then. He didn't want to forget anything from that day.

He flipped through the journal until he found the page he was looking for. The list was almost unreadable from all of the erasing and scratching out of words. Reading the names on the list made him feel like his twelve-year-old self. Sadly, he wanted to feel that way at that moment. He felt closer to his mother, because the older he became, the fuzzier the memories became.

After the bright memories faded, the dark thoughts moved in. Screams echoed in his head. The walls closed in on him as the screams became louder and louder. He could picture the wetness of her blood as it left her body and fell to the floor so distinctly. He was trapped in between four walls with nowhere to go. He battled the dark visions by forcing forward positive thoughts about his mother. His mind flashed pictures of her smiling down on him and her beautiful face next to his in a warm embrace.

He fell to his knees and prayed away all of the bad thoughts that ran through his mind. He talked to his mother during the prayer. She and God were the only ones that knew his torment. A word from her was all he needed but a response would never come. When he was done and he felt that he was ready to put on a brave face, he left the basement.

CHAPTER 23

Family members rushed in and out of the delivery room. Maya was finally in labor. She came from a big family, two brothers, and two sisters. They were all there, as well as her parents. Aunt Pearl, Starr, Loreal, Michelle, and their spouses were also in attendance. No one wanted to miss the birth.

King's and Maya's first born was a beautiful baby girl they named, Samiya. She went from one arm to the next, until the nurses had to take her to the nursery.

"I'm so proud of the two of you. This is just what you need, King. That little girl is going to melt your heart," Aunt Pearl said.

"She already has," he said.

"I saw those tears. Don't try to hide it," Starr teased, giving him a long hug. "Thanks for making me an auntie."

Starr gave Maya a hug.

"Isn't she beautiful? I can't believe she is finally here. I almost snatched her back from the nurse, because I want my baby right here with me," Maya said. The nurses were still monitoring her, so they ignored the comment and kept doing their job.

"Let the nurses get her all checked out and make sure she is healthy. She'll be back in here soon enough. Then, you gon' wish she was in the nursery," Aunt Pearl said with a big laugh.

King sat down on the side of the bed with Maya and rubbed her hand.

"I love you, baby," he said. "Thank you for my daughter."

"I love you, too, and you are welcome," Maya said.

It was late, well after midnight and everyone had gone home, except for Aunt Pearl and Starr.

"I'm going to get Aunt Pearl home. I know she's ready to go," King said, giving Maya a kiss on the cheek.

"You be here for your wife. Starr can take me home," she said.

"Umm, I didn't drive," Starr replied.

"You didn't walk, either. So, how were you getting home?" Aunt Pearl asked.

"My boyfriend dropped me off," Starr said.

"Boyfriend?" all three said in unison.

"Yes, my boyfriend," Starr said with emphasis.

"Oh my, this one must be special. I ain't never heard this child say boyfriend, but she sho' had many friends," Aunt Pearl said.

"Don't worry about it, I'm taking you home. She needs to get some rest and I want a drink after all of this," King said.

"Just promise me you won't get into any trouble with Richie and them. You're a father now and you don't need to get yourself caught up in other people's problems," Maya said.

"Baby, I know I'm a father now. I don't need you to tell me that. I'm not going to go out here and do something stupid to send me away from you, or our daughter. Trust me," King said.

"So Starr, when are we going to meet your new boyfriend?" Maya asked.

"Very soon. I'm just taking it slow," Starr replied.

"Come on, King. I'm ready to go now," Aunt Pearl said.

Starr stood to help her to her feet. She placed the walker in front of Aunt Pearl, who was readier than everyone thought. She was up and on her feet, heading for the door.

"Yes ma'am," he said, grabbing his keys and winking at Maya as he left. Starr stayed with Maya as she waited on her ride.

King led Aunt Pearl to the elevators. She moved slowly and carefully with each step. He was trying to get used to seeing her that way. She recently needed the help of a walker to get around. It was hard for him to watch her age, but she was still sharp as a pin. That kept him smiling.

"How have you been feeling?" he asked, as they stepped on the empty elevator.

"I'm just fine. It hurts to get this age you know. It don't hurt as bad as it looks," she said. She bellowed a deep laugh, one he hadn't heard in a very long time.

"You know, I worry about you sometimes. I don't know why you don't want to move back in the house. There's plenty of room with Starr gone. That way, I can keep an eye on you."

"That's exactly why I like my own place. I don't need you kids worrying about me, and all in my business. I done raised you and still providing a roof over your heads. Just let me be. I'm doing just fine where I am. I promise you that if that time comes and I'm blessed to know it, I will let you know that my days are numbered."

They reached the first floor, which was occupied hours earlier with people, but it was now empty except for a few. The elevator was across from the automatic doors. Aunt Pearl walked slowly over to the chairs, which lined the floor to ceiling windows that surrounded the waiting area. She lowered herself slowly into the chair nearest the automatic doors, positioning her body slowly to where she could see King pull up the car.

"Wait right here. I will be right back," he said.

"I'll see you when you come around," she said.

King stood there for a second, debating on asking his next question.

"What's the matter, son?" she asked, eyeing him.

"Are you sure you're all right? You seem like you're in pain."

"I am most days. These old bones dun' had it. I can't sit too long. I can't stand too long. It's just old age, son. I told you, I'm just fine. Now go on. I am ready to go home." She waved him off.

King gave her another once-over before leaving her. She smiled at him and shook her head. He blew her a kiss and exited the hospital. In the parking deck, he hit the button on his key chain to unlock the car doors. Headlights shone to the right of him as he walked to his car and dialed Richie.

"Hey man, what's up?" Richie asked.

"My baby girl is here!" King said with excitement.

A smile sat widely on his face as he thought about her. He opened the car door and cleaned out the car. A pink basket filled with baby items sat in the front passenger seat of the car. He removed the basket and placed it in the back.

"Congratulations, man! Welcome to fatherhood," Richie said.

"Thanks, she is so beautiful," King said.

"So, what's up? You trying to go out for a drink or Maya have you on lockdown?"

"Yeah, man I need a drink after all of this. I'm trying to go to the bar."

"Let's go. Are you on your way?"

"Yeah, I have to drop Auntie off first."

"Cool," Richie said. In the background, a female's angry voice penetrated the phone. "Hold on."

"Who is that?" King asked, with a frown.

"Sheneeta's crazy ass."

"Didn't I tell you I saw her and Roland at the doctor's office together, and you still dealing with her?"

"Naw, it ain't it like that."

"I thought you were done with her when she lied about you and four other dudes being her baby daddy," King said with a laugh.

"Go ahead, man. You got jokes. It ain't even like that."

"I'm on my way," King said, as he hung up his phone and pulled out of the parking deck. He pulled in front of the hospital and opened the passenger door. He went inside to help Aunt Pearl. He tried to help her up.

"I got it," she said.

"I know you do, but you taught me to be a gentleman," he said.

She sucked her teeth at him and rolled her eyes. Without letting go of her arm, he led her to the car, where she slid her frail body into the front seat. He placed her walker in the trunk.

"King, when I last went by the house, the grass was in patches. In all the years I lived there, I ain't never seen my grass like that. All the life around there is dying. That can't be a good sign. I don't know what you doing or what you plan on doing, but you better think about that little girl first. I don't like it at all. You and Starr better stop it while you still can. No good comes from evildoing. I knows it."

"Grass and plants die. That's what happens when it gets cold."

"No, son. That's a sign of death. The frost ain't here yet."

"Everything is fine. I promise you that."

On the ride home, it was quiet. It was late and she'd been at the hospital most of the day. He knew she was tired, so he didn't want to press her any further for conversation, especially the way the first one started out. She seemed so tired. She laid her head back on the headrest and closed her eyes. King turned the radio to the oldies, but goodies station for her enjoyment.

When they arrived at Aunt Pearl's apartment, he had to wake her. He shook her shoulders lightly. She lifted her head and opened her eyes. She looked around as if she didn't know where she was. She looked over at King.

"Oh, King. Did I fall I asleep?" she asked. She sat up quickly and unbuckled her seatbelt.

King walked her to her apartment and made sure she was safely inside. Before he left, she anointed him with anointing oil. She said a silent prayer between her and God. He kissed her and hugged her tightly as an unsettling feeling came over him. His gut told him to go back to the hospital with Maya and not to the bar with Richie. He fought off the uneasy feeling and drove to Richie's house.

CHAPTER 24

Richie and King arrived at the sports bar. There were pool tables, music, drinks, and food. It was a white stone building situated on a small lot; the parking lot held less than twenty cars. Although, many people didn't know about it, once found, it was a small treasure. Drinks were cheap and strong. There were a few tables for those who chose to occupy them. Not many people frequented the bar, but there was enough to have a nice weekend scene.

When Richie and King arrived, the parking lot was full. The only available parking was on the street. That meant the bar was packed. King found parking around the corner. It had been a few months since he had been there. With all the cars, more people must've found out about the place.

King and Richie tucked their guns in their backs without saying a word to each other. There were no security checks at the door, which made for a more dangerous environment.

When they arrived at the bar, they were surprised to see someone at the door checking for ID. There were about six people ahead of them. They watched as the bearded older gentleman checked each person's ID and let them in. He didn't wand or pat anyone down.

When it was King's turn, he pulled out his wallet and showed his ID. The man checked it and let him by. Richie did the same. Once inside, they saw why things were different. The place was packed with people. Music blared from the speakers, much different from their previous visits.

"Yo, that's Mike up there. I guess he's the DJ tonight," Richie shouted over the music.

"My man, Richie Rich and King, is in the building!" Mike shouted into the mic.

Heads turned towards the door. Bass ran through their bodies as they walked, unfazed, toward the bar.

"Damn, if the enemy is here they know we are, too," Richie said. He reached in his back and moved his gun closer to his side.

"I ain't worried about shit. I see a few fuck boys." King scanned the room, making eye contact when needed.

They both ordered a shot and beer. As the night went on, they greeted a few people they knew and continued drinking. After an hour, King reached his limit. He could feel his senses dull and everything moved in slow motion.

Richie was on the other side of the bar, out of King's vision. The last time he saw him, he was dancing with a young lady. King found a table and sat with a few guys he knew. He didn't drink anymore as he waited the alcohol out.

A commotion suddenly broke out on the dance floor. The thick crowd moved toward the door and women screamed. The music stopped. King realized that something bad was happening. He turned to his left as he saw people running his way. He quickly sobered up as his senses caught up with him; he looked for Richie, but didn't see him. The guys at the table all stood and headed for the door, but not before making sure that King didn't need them to stay.

The crowd cleared to where the fight was visible to the people at the bar and tables. Richie was fighting, along with Mike beside him. King quickly fought his way through the crowd to Richie's side. He stomped a man on the floor as Mike stood guard. Mike tossed a man into the wall and he didn't stand back up.

"What the fuck is going on?" King shouted. He watched Richie's back as he didn't know whom they were fighting. King had the urge to pull out his gun and shoot any man that approached them. Richie didn't respond; his adrenaline was pumping strong. He kept right on kicking and stomping the man on the floor.

"Come on!" King said. He pulled Richie off the man. He pushed King off him and almost hit him. "What the hell are you doing? Let's go!" King said.

A few spectators stood around, watching. The bar's employees finally made their way to where they were.

"Get out of here and don't come back! The police are on the way," a man said, with a shotgun pointed at the floor.

"We're leaving," King said, with his hands in the air. He pulled Richie behind him.

"I should kill your ass! Fuck you!" Richie spat at the man on the floor.

Outside was a small crowd of people. Cars left the parking lot and backed up traffic. They had a little ways to walk. King didn't know whom Richie was fighting and who else they had to look out for. They walked toward the street where the car was parked on the corner. They moved swiftly, with a few others walking to their cars.

He looked back at Richie. He wiped his bloody nose and straightened his clothes.

"Richie," someone called from behind them.

When King turned around, he saw Richie turn toward the person. A shot was fired and Richie spun around, stumbling backward. King saw Roland; he reached in his back, pulled out his gun, and fired at Roland. Just as Roland let off another shot at Richie, he was hit in the chest. He grabbed his chest and now aimed at King, who pulled the trigger again, sending a bullet into Roland's head. King kicked himself mentally for not remembering headshots only; he now understood why.

When the gunfire ended, King was shaking and his ears ringing. He looked down at Richie, who sat against a car, bleeding from his mouth and stomach. He kneeled down beside him.

"Richie, it's okay, man," King said. He placed his hand against Richie's stomach as blood spilled between his fingers. "Don't talk, just hang in there. Keep breathing," he said.

Richie coughed up blood when he tried to talk. He tried to speak once again, but choked on his blood.

King heard people running towards them and he pointed his gun in the direction of the footsteps.

"Get out of here, King. I got this!" Mike said. He knelt down beside King. Mike pulled out a cell phone.

"Shots fired. Two shooting victims. Requesting immediate backup and medical..." Mike said. He reached into his shirt and pulled out a badge hanging from his neck as he continued to speak. He pushed King away from Richie and applied pressure to his stomach with a shirt.

"What is this? You're the police?" King asked in shock. He had no idea that his childhood friend was a police officer.

"I'm telling you to get the fuck out of here!" Mike said.

"I'm not leaving him. He's my brother!" King shouted, moving in closer to Richie.

"Get him out of here!" Mike said to a man standing behind him.

King stood weakly to his feet as he was dragged to his car. Before leaving, he saw Roland's lifeless body spilling a pool of blood on the sidewalk.

CHAPTER 25

When Tone arrived at the hospital to pick up Starr, he didn't come alone. He was with his mother, who was visiting from New York. Tone had a few beers and his mother refused to let him get behind the wheel. It was Starr's first time meeting anyone's parents. Tone's jealousy was much better than before. He was loving and caring towards her, even after she told him that she was unable to conceive. His feelings didn't change towards her.

"Baby, it was so nice meeting your mother. She is so gorgeous. I see where you get your good looks," Starr said. She plopped down onto the sofa and kicked off her heels. Tone sat down, lifted her feet on his lap, and rubbed them without her asking.

"See, you are just too good for me. You know me so well. Trust, my feet are killing me," she said. She sat back and closed her eyes to enjoy the foot massage.

"I have something that I need to talk to you about," Tone said.

Starr's eyes opened wide and she shot straight up. "What do you need to talk to me about?" she asked nervously. She hoped that no one told him about her past that she tried to bury.

"You know how I told you that I did some stupid things back in the day. I spent so long running from my past," he said. He continued to rub her feet as he spoke.

"Just tell me. We all have a past. I've done things that I'm not proud of. You can tell me anything."

"When I was younger and lived here in Richmond, I committed a horrible crime. My parents found me covered in blood, and talking to myself in our bathroom. That was when we moved back to New York. They never turned me in. I spent years telling a psychiatrist everything except the truth, about what really happened."

A chill ran up Starr's spine as an eerie feeling crept into the room. She watched as he rubbed her stiff feet and looked out into space as he spoke.

"What did you do?" she asked. She wanted to know what crime he committed, but then she didn't want to know.

"I killed a woman. She was the most beautiful woman I'd ever seen. It was something special about her. No one noticed except me. She wasn't my age and I knew she wouldn't be interested in me. Somehow I got it in my mind that she would."

"Didn't you tell me you lived in K.C.?" As her mind placed the pieces to the puzzle together, the picture became clear.

He stopped rubbing her feet. Her heart skipped a beat.

"Starr, I love you. I really don't want this to come between us. I was young and stupid back then. When you're a kid, you do dumb things. I'm a man now. I'm not the same person I was back then," he said.

Starr looked at him in disgust. Tears formed in her eyes as the reality of her newfound lover being Jasmine's killer. What was the chance of that happening?

"Tell me you aren't talking about King's mother? Tell me you didn't do it! Tell me! I need to hear you say it!" she shouted. She swung her feet to the floor and looked him in the eyes.

Tone met her gaze. Took her by the hand and slid in closer to her. He wiped her tears as they fell one by one down her cheeks.

"Baby, I'm telling you this, because I love you. I want to spend the rest of my life with you. I felt that this was something that I needed to get off my chest first. When you told me he was your brother, I wanted to leave. I knew that would hurt you. It's not like he's your real brother, anyway," he said.

"Did you kill his mother?"

"I made a mistake when I was younger. I didn't mean to hurt her."

"You killed her! How could you hurt someone like her? She didn't pose you any harm. Why?"

"I told you, I was infatuated with her. I thought I was in love with her and she would love me back. I had issues back then."

He pounded his fist against his forehead. Starr was scared.

"I live with what I did every day. I punish myself for what I did."

Starr pushed away from him. She walked to the window and looked down to the street as she tried to digest what he was saying.

"Get out! I can't see you anymore," she said.

"What?" He walked behind her.

175

"I said get out! Don't you ever call me or come here again! Do you understand me?"

"Please, baby, I love you. I'm sorry for what I did. I'm not the same person I was back then."

"I don't know who you are. But I know there is no way we could be together after this," she said. "Now get out!" She sobbed.

Tone backed away from her with tears forming in his eyes. He walked out the door.

Starr fell to her knees and sobbed. It felt as if she was punished all over again. Happiness was something else she couldn't achieve. Real love came, disguised as a murderer. Just when she thought she found happiness, it was snatched away from her by the truth. Being the good Starr didn't work out for her. She didn't see the benefit other than having her heart broken.

A knock on the door broke her out of her pity party. She didn't move. She didn't want to see Tone's face ever again. He put her in a bad predicament.

"Starr, open the door!" a voice shouted from the other side.

Her head snapped as she recognized King's voice. She jumped to her feet and ran to the door. She quickly wiped away her tears with her hands. She swung open the door.

"King, what are you doing here? Where have you been?" she asked.

"I fucked up, Starr," he said, falling into her arms.

He could barely stand on his own two feet. She dragged him to the sofa. He could barely walk or talk. When he opened his mouth to talk, she knew why. He was drunk as a skunk.

"Oh, my God! What have you been drinking?" Starr asked. She laid him down on the sofa and rushed into the kitchen for the trash can. Carefully she placed the can near his head that hung off the sofa.

"Don't move! I'm going to call, Maya," she said. "Make sure if you get sick, please, use the trash can. It's right here." She placed his hand on the can so that he knew exactly where it was. She ran back to the kitchen and dialed Maya's number.

"Maya, King is here at my house. He just showed up drunk. I don't know where he came from, but he is drunk. I just wanted to let you know. As soon as he sobers up, I will find out what's going on," she said.

She took his keys and took his shoes off. When she was done, she went back to bed to finish questioning God.

Why did things turn out the way they did? Just when I thought I found love, it wasn't. Why me? Why can't I be happy?

She missed Tone already. She'd become used to sleeping in his arms most nights. The nights when they were apart, she yearned for him.

CHAPTER 26

It was morning and the sun shined brightly through the windows. The streets below were quiet outside of Starr's apartment. The usual hustle and bustle to and from local establishments were at a minimum.

King rolled over and almost fell off the sofa. Catching himself, he sat up in the dark. His head hurt. He rubbed his eyes and looked around the room. He didn't know where he was. He looked down at the coffee table and saw a picture in a frame. He picked up the picture and looked at it closely. It was a picture of Starr and a familiar face. He immediately recognized Tone from the picture.

"It's about time you woke up. You need to call Maya. You have a hell of a lot of explaining to do," she said. She handed him a cup of coffee. "Drink this," she said.

She took a seat on the adjacent chair. She sipped her coffee and studied him.

"How in the hell did I make it over here?" he asked. He pressed his face into his hands in a downward motion.

"What the hell happened? I heard Richie was shot last night and you were with him."

King took a deep breath and laid his head back on the sofa. He looked at his hands that had dried blood on them. He ran to the bathroom and scrubbed his hands.

"I saw that, mister," she called out after him.

He didn't respond. He came back in the living room with a towel around his neck and shirtless. "Give me one of your boyfriend's shirts," he said rudely.

Starr turned her nose up at him and sat her cup of coffee down on the table. She went to get him a shirt. She threw a striped shirt at him.

"Who is that in the picture with you?" he asked. He pulled the shirt over his head.

"What picture?" she asked.

"Don't play stupid. Who is that in the picture? Don't tell me that's your new boyfriend," he said, pointing at the coffee table.

"No, we aren't dating anymore."

"Yesterday, he was your boyfriend."

"I don't want to talk about it. We are not together now. He's a liar like the rest of you men," she said. She felt that it was the right time to reveal what she learned, but she couldn't bring herself to do it.

"That dude has some issues. He used to look at my mother all crazy and shit.

He acted like my daddy. He looked out for me, but I knew something wasn't right with him," he said.

Starr sat nervously as King spoke.

"Just so you know, he is on my list of suspects. Number three as a matter of fact," he said.

"Boy, leave me alone about him," she said nervously.

"I've been looking for him. Now he's back in town after all these years," he said.

He looked at Starr as if she knew something. She continued to sip her hot coffee and scroll through her cell phone. She dialed Maya's number.

"Here, talk to your wife," she said, handing King the phone.

She went into her bedroom and closed the door behind her. Her heart raced as she fought the urge to tell him what she knew, but she didn't want him to do something stupid. He had too much to lose. She also still loved Tone and didn't want to see anything happen to him. She felt so guilty for withholding information from King. In all the years, she'd never done something like that to him. She knew that if he found out, he would be crushed. They vowed always to have each other's back, no matter what. She looked at herself in the mirror and saw a lying, conniving woman staring back at her.

King walked into her bedroom without knocking.

"You should knock first," she said, quickly turning towards him.

"I'm about to go to the hospital. I hope you're not sleeping with the enemy. After seeing that picture of him, something's not sitting right with me," he said, tossing her phone at her. "Once I get my head clear, I'll deal with it."

Ignoring his comment, she sucked her teeth. "What happened last night with Richie? I know you were there," she said.

"My best friend was killed last night and I killed the man that killed him," he said. He turned and walked out.

Starr's jaw fell open as King admitted to killing someone. She didn't think he had it in him. She didn't put anything past him, either. She let out a sigh of relief that she didn't tell him about Tone. She sat on her bed in shock. King changed right before her eyes, and it was ugly.

CHAPTER 27

King arrived at the hospital to an angry Maya. She was worried sick about him since he didn't return to the hospital. When she received the call that Richie was shot, she feared that he was hurt. When he walked into the hospital room with a hangover and noticed the room filled with angry faces, he dropped his head in shame.

"Hi, everybody," he said.

He stood in front of Maya's bed. Dry hellos came from Maya's mother, father, and Aunt Pearl.

"I know you all are probably upset with me. I'm sorry for worrying you. I need to talk to my wife," he said.

Maya's parents were the first to leave the room without a word. Her father brushed against King on his way out. He knew he deserved it and didn't respond.

"You should be ashamed of yourself. You are starting this thing out all wrong. Your wife just had your baby and she is stressed out over you. I found out about Richie's death from the news. I know you were with him. The least you could've done was call," Aunt Pearl said.

"I know and I'm sorry. Please, let me talk to my wife alone," he asked.

"You don't have to tell me twice," she said. She struggled to her feet. King rushed over to help her.

"Maya, I'm right outside this door if you need me," she said, rolling her eyes at King.

After everyone had left, King and Maya were alone. Maya's eyes were puffy and red. He walked over, hugged and kissed her. They both cried; Richie was a friend of them both.

"You had me calling the hospitals and jails! I didn't know what happened to you. I've never been so scared in my life. I just had your baby! How could you put me through that?" Maya said, between sobs.

"Baby, I'm so sorry. I didn't mean to hurt you," he said.

"I'm sorry about Richie. I don't know what happened, but I am glad that you are safe," she said.

They held each other and found comfort. Just then, the nurse came in with the baby, and Samiya's presence changed the sour mood in the room. Both of their faces lit up.

"Is this a good time?" the nurse asked.

"Yes, it is perfect timing," King said.

He picked up his baby girl and held her close. The bond he felt with her was more powerful than he could've ever imagined. She made all of his worries go away.

"I'm sorry you didn't get to meet your Uncle Richie. Just know that he loved you, baby girl."

Samiya cooed as he spoke to her. She looked at him as if she knew exactly what he was talking about. He rocked her in his arms.

"She smiled at me!" he said. He held the baby so that Maya could see her face. Maya smiled.

"That's crazy! She's not even a day old and she already smiling at her daddy," he said proudly. "Now, I know that everything is going to be all right."

"She passed her hearing test today. I knew you were worried about her being deaf. Right now, we are out of the water, but she will need to be retested by a trained audiologist when she turns one. They want to retest since she is at risk, because of your mother's condition."

"Thank God! I already knew she was going to be fine." He kissed his daughter.

"I've been up all night worrying about you. I'm exhausted and my blood pressure is up. If I fall asleep on you, please, don't leave me," she said. She yawned and rubbed her red, swollen eyes.

"Baby, don't worry. I'm not going anywhere."

"Okay, I love you."

"I love you, too."

Maya kissed King and Samiya. The nurse administered her medication so she could rest. Aunt Pearl and Maya's parents re-entered the room.

"Is everything okay in here?" Maya's mother asked.

"Yes, ma'am. Again, I apologize," he said.

"The good thing is that you're fine. I'm sorry about your friend," Maya's father said. "It's time to grow up and leave those streets alone. You're a husband and father now. I've been there, son. I lost a lot of friends to the streets," her father said. He patted King on the back.

"Somebody needs to talk some sense into him. I knew something bad was going to happen. That's why I prayed for you," Aunt Pearl said. "Bring my baby over here."

Without protest, King handed Samiya to Aunt Pearl. He didn't want her to leave his arms. She was warm and so innocent.

"Hand me a diaper and one of those bottles. You can have her back when I'm done," she said.

"Since Maya's resting, we're going to go. Let her know that we'll see her later. We'll bring dinner by for everyone," Maya's mother said.

"Thanks," King said.

"You don't plan on leaving, do you?" her father asked.

"No, sir. I will be right here," he said.

"Great. Well, we'll see you all at dinnertime," he said.

Her parents left after kissing Aunt Pearl and Samiya goodbye. Aunt Pearl was livid with King. He could tell, because she couldn't look at him and spoke harshly towards him. He could say sorry a million times and that wouldn't change a thing with her. He knew that she loved him and probably had thought the worse. He felt guilty for putting them through the torment of not knowing if he was dead or alive.

CHAPTER 28

Two days later, Maya and Samiya were released from the hospital. Samiya was a healthy baby girl and ready to go home. Maya was released as well, but her blood pressure had to be monitored. King felt he was the reason for her recent health issue.

At home, Aunt Pearl had everything ready for their return home. She'd prepared a home-cooked meal, washed all the baby's clothes, and sterilized the bottles. When they returned home, they didn't need to do anything.

"Welcome home!" Aunt Pearl said. She greeted them with open arms. "Maya, I have everything taken care of. All you need to do is rest and take care of that baby. I will do everything else."

Maya walked in, with the baby wrapped tightly in a receiving blanket. King was loaded down with an overnight bag and diaper bag.

"Thank you so much. I don't know what we would do without you. Neither King nor I really know what to expect now that we have to care for her on our own," Maya said.

"Thanks, Auntie," King said. He put down the bags he carried. He hugged her tightly and kissed her.

"You're welcome. Hand me that baby," Aunt Pearl said.

"I'm capable of taking care of my baby. I know I'm a first-time mom, but I know I can do it if you'll let me!" Maya shouted. She held Samiya closer to her.

King and Aunt Pearl looked at her as if she lost her mind. Maya stared back at them. She took in a deep breath and handed the baby to Aunt Pearl. She looked to King, and then Aunt Pearl.

"Umm, I do need a hot shower. I'll get her when I'm done," she said. She walked away.

"I'm not trying to take over. I'm just here to help. I dun' raised all mine, so you don't have to worry about that," Aunt Pearl said, looking after Maya suspiciously.

When Maya left the room, Aunt Pearl motioned for King to come closer.

"You keep an eye on that girl. She might have the pregnancy depression," she whispered.

"Yeah, she's been tripping the last couple of days. The doctor talked to us about post-partum depression before we left the hospital. Don't worry, I will keep an eye on her," he said.

"Yeah, that's what you call it," she said.

Aunt Pearl proceeded to change Samiya's diaper and fed her. She wanted to give her a proper bath, but decided to let Maya and King give her the first bath. King unpacked their bags and gave Maya some privacy by staying out of her way. She was quiet and reserved. After her shower, she joined Aunt Pearl.

"I'm so sorry for speaking to you that way. My emotions have been all over the place. I'm worried about

King, and with Richie being killed, I've just been in a really bad place," Maya explained.

"It's all right. It's going to take some time for you to feel like yourself again. Don't let that boy worry you. All you need to worry about is this bundle of joy right here," Aunt Pearl said. She placed Samiya in her mother's arms. That put a smile on Maya's face.

Knock . . . knock . . . knock!

There was a heavy knock on the door. Both Maya and Aunt Pearl looked at each other. King rushed from the bedroom.

"Go in the back and don't come out until I tell you!" he said.

He helped Aunt Pearl to her feet who didn't have anything to say back. She rushed behind Maya to the back of the house.

King was scared. He knew eventually that the police would come to question him about Richie's murder. He didn't know which side Mike was really on, but after finding out he was a police officer, he tried not to think about it. However, he knew that he didn't want to be handcuffed in front of his family.

Knock . . . knock . . . knock!

King looked out the window. He only saw cars parked on the street. There wasn't a police car in sight. He took a deep breath and opened the door.

"What's up, King," Mike said. He was in his usual attire, a black tee, baggy jeans, and latest sneakers.

With a laugh, King said, "Oh, so you hood today, but you really a pig!"

"I deserve that, that's why I'm here. I just want to talk to you. No badge. No gun," Mike said, holding up his hands.

As much as King wanted to slam the door in his face, he needed to hear what he had to say. They'd both lost a friend; it felt as if he lost Mike as a friend too, and it hurt. It wasn't just the fact that he was a police officer, but the fact that he didn't tell him. He thought they were closer than that. They grew up together, played together, and should've been closer than that.

"You have five minutes, man," King said, backing away from the door.

Mike walked into the house. He looked around at the baby carrier and other items in the living room. "Oh, yeah, congratulations!" he said.

"Thanks," King said dryly.

"Look, I'm sorry I didn't tell you and Richie I was a cop. I didn't see why I should blow my cover when neither one of you was on my radar. We were just three kids coming up in the projects and I made it out. No matter what, I always had your back," he said.

"I thought we were bigger than that. You were in my wedding," King said. "That's some shit I needed to know."

"At some point, you would've found out. I'm new to this, too. You know better than anybody how the streets of Richmond operate, man. Drugs have infested our streets for too long. We are losing our people to this shit. I want to do something to help my city, even if it's behind the shield." Mike said.

"Look how it came out! Right there in front of our dying friend!" King shouted.

"You're right, and again, I'm sorry," Mike said. "I came to let you know that you don't have anything to worry about. I took care of everything. Roland shot Richie and Richie shot Roland," Mike said.

"Yeah, but we both know that's not what happened," King said.

"I didn't see you shoot anybody. I came on the scene and found two men shot to death," Mike said.

King thought about what he said. "So, what I owe you now?"

"No, we're squared," Mike said.

"Yeah, thanks," he said.

Mike held out his hand in front of King. King hesitated for a moment, before grabbing his hand and pulling in for a manly embrace.

"King, is it all right to come out?" Maya asked, peeking her head around the corner.

"Yeah," King said.

"Oh, hi Mike. You were knocking like the police. Scared us half to death," Maya said.

Mike walked to Maya and gave her a hug.

"Did you come to see the baby?" she asked.

Mike looked back at King. King nodded his approval.

"Yeah, where is she?" he asked.

Maya led Mike to the nursery where Samiya was sleeping. King took two beers from the refrigerator. He joined Maya and Mike in the nursery.

CHAPTER 29

The day of Richie's funeral was tough for everyone, especially his mother. King went to Richie's house to meet with the family before the funeral. She'd known him for so long that she called King her son when she introduced him to people. She was there the day his mother died, and he wanted to be there for her.

"Thanks for coming. I really wanted you to ride with the family. You were like a brother to him," Ms. Bowling said. She hugged him tightly.

People were everywhere. Some were still getting dressed and others were in the kitchen, putting out food on the table.

"Hello, everyone," King said politely. Richie's mother still held on to him.

"Richie didn't want a big funeral. He always told me that. He didn't want us crying over his dead body. He wants all of us to remember him in life. I'm going to honor his wishes and lay him to rest the way he wanted," she said.

"Okay, I know that whatever you do, Richie would be proud," he said.

"We're going to be at the gravesite. The pastor is going to speak and we can all say our goodbyes. It will be a closed casket, so don't expect to see him. I had one of his good pictures blown up for the service," she said. She sobbed a little. King rubbed her back and led her to a nearby chair.

"I just can't believe he is gone. My baby is gone." She pulled out a tissue and wiped away her tears. "Lord, knows he is in a better place. That's the only thing that's getting me through this," she said.

King fought back tears as a lump formed in his throat. It hurt to see her grieve for her son and his friend. It was senseless that he died over a female and a baby that probably wasn't his.

"That girl, Sheneeta, keep on calling, talking about Richie was her baby daddy. He told me he wasn't. I heard that there were several other possibilities. I don't know what to do about that," she said.

"Don't worry about that today. Let's put Richie to rest," he said.

The graveside service was very emotional for everyone. Richie's mother held it together, until it was time to leave. Sheneeta made a scene, falling all over the casket. Someone had to pull her off before she and the casket fell six feet under.

King spoke to a few people he hadn't seen in many years and they all gave their condolences. While walking back to the family car with Richie's mother, Gooch tapped him on his shoulder.

"I need to talk to you," Gooch said. Gooch was behind dark shades, and dressed in a black suit.

King was startled. He didn't know if Gooch wanted answers to Richie's death, or if he was there on business.

"Go ahead, King," Ms. Bowling said. "Are we going to see you back at the house? We have room in the car if you need a ride, Gooch."

"I'll be there, sister," Gooch said. Richie's mom got in the car. Gooch led King to the side. "You okay?" Gooch asked. No smile, no expression.

"I'm good, because Roland's mother is feeling the same pain she's feeling," King said. He gestured towards Ms. Bowling.

"Good looking out. I heard what you did; thank you. You saved me a bullet. I have some news for you. I have that information you've been seeking."

"What? Who is it?"

Knots formed in King's stomach.

"Number three. He was seen running home all bloody and shit. The problem is, that was the last time he was seen. His family packed up and moved out that very day. That's all I have for you."

Gooch walked away, leaving King standing alone. A horn blared and brought him out of a state of shock. He walked briskly back to the car to join Richie's family. Gears turned and plots formed as he planned his revenge. He was unchained.

CHAPTER 30

Starr arrived at King's and Maya's house; the house where she grew up. She'd been avoiding King, because she felt guilty about not telling him Tone was responsible for his mother's death.

She'd cried herself to sleep at night, beating herself up for falling in love with an obsessed murderer. She tried to find a way to tell King without him killing her and Tone. None of the scenarios played out in her favor. Either way, King could end up in prison. She reached in the back seat for the gift bag full of outfits she'd purchased for Samiya when her car door swung open.

"What are you doing?" Starr asked.

"Get out the car, Starr!" King shouted.

"What the hell is wrong with you?"

He was fuming with anger. His nostrils flared and his eyebrows appeared to be one. When she didn't move fast enough for him, he yanked her out the car by the arm.

"Get your damn hands off of me!" she shouted. She tried to pull away from him.

"You know, don't you?" he asked. He pushed her back against the car.

"I don't know what you're talking about! Get off of me!"

He pressed harder against her. He peered down on her. "You're such a bad liar. You can't even look me in my face."

He slowly backed away when her tears fell from her eyes and guilt danced in her face.

"I didn't know what he did. When I found out, I broke it off with him. I haven't seen or talked to him since, I swear to you. I just didn't know how to tell you. You and Maya are so happy. You have Samiya now. I didn't want you to throw all of that away on him!"

"You're sleeping with the enemy. My enemy! He's dead! You hear me!"

"I'm so sorry. Let the police handle it. Please, don't do something stupid that you would regret!" She ran behind him.

He turned to her. "If you felt the police could handle it, how come you didn't call?"

Starr stopped running behind him.

"You were supposed to be my sister. Nothing or no one was supposed to come between us. Always have each other's back, right?" he asked.

"Yes, but I just didn't know how to tell you," she sobbed.

"You're not welcome here," he said.

King walked back to the house and closed the door. She wanted to run to the front door and beg him to forgive her. She needed him to understand where she was coming from. If only he could listen to her, they would be able to work it out. Starr stood outside, crying for a few minutes, before she got in her car and drove off.

From inside the house, Maya watched the fight between Starr and King. As soon as he entered the house, she interrogated him.

"What was all that about?" Maya asked.

"Just stay out of it. This is between me and Starr," King said, pushing past her.

"What is going on with you? Lately, you've been walking around here as if you want to hurt somebody. Is it something I did?" she asked.

"No. Just don't worry about it. Starr is dead to me; she betrayed me."

"I invited her over to see Samiya. I didn't know things were that serious between you two." She wrapped her arms around him.

"Believe me, it's that bad. Just respect what I said."

"I never tried to come in between you two, but you need to work things out with her. Life is too short for you two to keep this foolishness going."

"I know, but this time, she fucked up."

Baby Samiya cried out from her nursery. Maya walked away from King. "I'll get her."

"No, you sit down. I'll get her this time," he said, pulling her back to him. He kissed her deeply. "I love you."

After King fed Samiya and put her back to sleep, he and Maya watched a movie and cuddled on the sofa. Many times, he felt he needed to tell her that he knew who killed his mother. He wanted her to tell him to do the right thing, needed her to tell him to call the police and report what he knew. He would definitely tell them to talk to Starr for additional information. He contemplated his next step. Starr was the link to Tone and without her, Tone's trail was cold.

CHAPTER 31

King sat outside Starr's apartment for three hours, waiting for her to return home. He ran to the pizza shop to grab a slice of pizza and soda. Twice he had to run inside to use the restroom. It was cold outside and as the time went by, the cooler it became.

Twenty minutes later, Starr pulled into her assigned parking space. She was alone, just what he had hoped. She popped her trunk and retrieved several shopping bags. He had to confront her and find out which side she was on, because he needed her. He opened the car door and jogged up to her.

"Hey, Starr," he said.

"Oh, my God! You scared me. You shouldn't be running up on people like that!" she said, as she closed the trunk of her car. "What do you want?"

"I wanted to apologize," King said.

"No, first let me say that I'm so sorry for not telling you about Tone. I don't know how you found out, but I'm glad you did. I was wrong, but know that I wasn't trying to protect him," she said.

"I know you were trying to protect me, I felt that you chose him over me. You still should've told me, no matter the outcome," he said. "You need some help with those bags?"

Starr smiled and handed two of the bags to King and headed to her apartment. She put away her groceries, while King flipped through channels on the television.

"So, what are we going to do about your boy?" he asked.

Starr walked into the living room and sat down beside him. "That's just what I was thinking. I haven't talked to him since the day he confessed. He really thought I was going to stay with him after that."

"That dude was sick. I always knew something wasn't right with him. You better be glad he didn't do anything to you."

"I thanked God for that. I won't lie; I really fell in love with him."

"I need to know everything you know about him. Addresses, phone numbers, what car he drives, everything."

"I got you. What's the plan? Are we going to the police? I have a friend we can call."

"No, he is going to pay with his life."

"So are you, if things go wrong. Are you sure you are willing to risk losing your wife and child?"

"It's not going to go wrong. I got this."

"Just let me know what you need me to do and I'll do it. Please be careful," she pleaded with him.

King ran his hand over her curly hair, making it messier. She hugged him.

"I missed you so much! You know I hate when we fight like this. I really thought you wrote me off this time," she said.

"I did for a minute, but I needed you," he said jokingly.

He went over his plan with Starr. His plan was to ambush him at home. Starr didn't feel right about letting him go through with it. If his plan went his way, he would kill Tone and possibly spend the rest of his life in prison or die. Although, she didn't have anything to do with his mother's death, she felt responsible for the way things turned out. If she hadn't dated Tone, King still wouldn't have known who his mother's murderer was.

There was no way she could let King ruin his life. The only way to end it was to have Tone pay for his sins, and she had to do that without involving King. She had to think of something fast. She went to what she knew best and called Agent Mosley.

CHAPTER 32

Starr sat at a table by the window in a local downtown diner. She read the paper as she waited for her guest to arrive. Several times, she picked up her phone to make sure she didn't miss a phone call or text.

She saw Tone crossing the street. She was surprisingly unnerved at seeing him. She didn't feel anything for him. She hated him, which made the meeting easier. He appeared nervous when he came to a complete stop at the front door. She watched him stop and look around on the street. *Don't get scared now, jerk,* she thought.

He peeked through the glass door. Starr then pretended not to see him and looked down at the newspaper and at her watch. She could feel him watching her. When a minute went by and he still didn't enter, she couldn't risk him leaving. She looked up from the newspaper and towards the door. He still watched her. With one small motion, she waved at him and smiled as if she was happy to see him.

"Come on in," she mumbled under her breath. "You crazy bastard."

Tone let a woman leave out the door, and then he came inside the diner. He looked around, paranoid. He walked slowly over to her table, and she stood to greet him. He hugged her before she had a chance to say a word.

"I missed you so much. I knew you would come around," Tone said.

"Umm, I missed you, too," she managed to say.

She pulled back from him and straightened her dress. She stepped back, bumping into the table and spilling over her coffee.

"Are you okay?" Tone asked suspiciously.

"I'm fine. It's just that it's been awhile," she said, as she sat down in her chair. "Please, have a seat."

Before sitting, he took one last look around the diner. "I wasn't sure if you wanted to see me or if you were trying to set me up." He leaned in closer to her and asked, "You didn't tell anybody that thing I told you about, did you?"

She wanted to scream, *Hell yeah and you're going to pay!* Instead, she smiled and put on a show.

"I've been thinking. Maybe I was too quick to judge you. You just caught me off guard and I didn't know how to respond to that," she said.

"I thought you would've been able to see past that," he said.

"See past what?" she asked, sipping her coffee. It was cold, but she pretended it was still hot.

"You know, that thing I told you about," he whispered.

"I just want to be sure that we're talking about the same thing."

"You know...about me hurting somebody when I was younger."

"King's mother right? And, let's be honest, she died."

"Yes. I don't want to talk about that. Let's just move forward. You didn't call me down here to talk about that. I was thinking, we should go back to your place and make up for lost time," he said.

"That sounds like a good idea. Why don't you stop and get a bottle of wine and meet me at my place," she said seductively.

"Okay," he said. He stood to his feet.

"Go ahead, let me finish my coffee first," she said, waving him on.

Tone left the diner with a big smile. After she had watched him cross the street, she picked up her cell phone.

"Hello? Hello? Did you get that? Please tell me that was enough?" she said.

"They heard him loud and clear," Agent Mosley said. "Just sit tight. We have a few formalities before we can issue this warrant. We have a judge on standby. You're safe. We have officers nearby."

"Okay," she said. She hung up the phone.

Starr took a deep breath. She finally did something selfless. After hearing King's plan, she decided to come up with a plan of her own. She called Agent Mosley and explained the dilemma. RPD helped arrange a meeting between Starr and Tone in hopes to get enough evidence for an arrest. She purposely left King in the dark about the RPD involvement. She only told him about the meet with Tone at the diner downtown. She'd told him she would record Tone's confession in case things went bad, so there would be proof.

CHAPTER 33

King watched Starr and Tone from the opposite side of the street. He wanted to fire bullets straight through the glass window and into Tone's head. He needed to be patient. He saw that Tone parked in a parking lot on a less busy street than the one the diner was on. That was where he chose to kill him.

King watched Tone cross the street to the parking lot. He was only five paces behind him and Tone didn't notice him in the crowd that moved across the street with him. To King, he didn't look much different than he did back then. Tone still wore cornrows neat and straight to the back, secured by black rubber bands at the ends. As always, he was dressed in army fatigue pants and black boots. It didn't matter the season, his wardrobe never changed. He was used to the up north chill and never really adjusted to the weather in Virginia.

Tone, still paranoid, looked around before stepping into his car. The crowd that King had blended in with now left him exposed as each person went their separate ways.

Tone started the car, but didn't close the door. He sat inside with his feet outside the car, finishing a Black and Mild. King could smell the smoke from the tobacco as he approached from three cars behind.

As King came closer, a wave of courage came over him. He wanted him to gaze upon his face before he killed him. He remembered Tone and was sure Tone would remember him, too. Tone plucked the remainder of his Black and Mild to the ground. The driver's side door was closing as King approached. He walked to the driver's side window and tapped on the glass, as Tone was buckling his seat belt. He didn't recognize King immediately, so he rolled down the window.

When the window was half way down and Tone was about to speak, King lifted his right hand and put a .357 Magnum through the window. Tone's eyes crossed as he looked at the gun against the middle of his forehead.

King had a choice to make in those seconds. The choice to let the man who'd caused him so much pain over the years, stand before twelve and be judged for his crimes. Alternatively, he could blow his brains all over his filthy car for taking his mother away from him

King saw red. He saw the red of the blood that stained the floors and walls. He saw the distinct bloody shoeprints that led from his mother's bedroom, down the stairs, through the living room, kitchen and out the back door. A choice had to be made and fast.

"King, no! Don't do it!" Starr shouted from a distance. He heard her and wanted to turn in the direction that she was shouting, but he didn't want Tone to get the upper hand. He stood firm. "The police are going to arrest him. We got him!" she called out. He could hear her moving quickly towards them.

He looked towards Starr for one split second. "No, he killed my mother! I'm not letting him get away, not this time!" King shouted. He focused back on Tone.

"This is your chance right here. Don't do it. Don't ruin your life over this. What about your daughter? She's going to need you, King. Don't let her grow up like the two of us," Starr pleaded.

King's finger was on the trigger, gun aimed, and he was ready to fire. He was sure just seconds before that all he wanted was to kill Tone, and then he thought about his daughter. Her beautiful smile flashed in his mind. The overwhelming feeling of love flooded him as he thought about being separated from her. Then, the darkness crept in as always, crowding his mind of images from his past and pushing all rational thoughts aside. He looked at Starr.

POW! POW!

Gunfire rang out. King didn't know where it came from, so he fired into the car several times, while moving towards Starr's direction. He caught a glance of Tone waving a pistol and holding his hand over his chest.

"Get down!" King shouted.

Bullets whizzed past King as he tried to take cover and get to Starr. He fired back in the direction of the bullets. After ducking behind a vehicle, he saw Starr on the ground between two cars. When he reached her, she was on her back. Police cars sped towards them and officers jumped out with guns pointed. King dropped his weapon and put his hands in the air.

"Don't shoot! My sister needs help!" he shouted.

"You bitch!" Tone shouted. He charged towards Starr and King with his gun in hand, spilling blood.

More gunshots rang out as King covered Starr with his body. When the gunfire ceased, Tone was dead. At least half of the bullets met its target. Officers rushed in and slammed King on the concrete, cuffing him. Others attended to Starr. They placed King in the back of a police car and he was taken to the station. He watched the chaotic scene until it was out of his sight.

EPILOGUE

Three months passed since the ordeal. Due to the special circumstances of the case, along with Mike and Agent Mosley vouching for him, King received a blessing and only served ninety days in the city jail for brandishing a firearm. All other charges were dropped after a plea agreement with the Commonwealth Attorney. The attorney Maya hired was worth his weight in gold; everything he said he would do, he came through.

Starr recovered from her injuries. She was shot in the shoulder and suffered a concussion when she fell to the ground. The bullet went through, not requiring surgery and no bones were broken. She was thankful that she only suffered a minor injury with all of the bullets that were flying around. With her near death experience, Starr woke up in the hospital, finally realizing her purpose in life. She didn't survive those many years ago to inflict pain on others. She didn't make it through her last brush with death to continue on the same path. She had a higher purpose. The things that she suffered through were only a test. She was a strong woman who had a testimony. She could share her story and show others that you can survive the worst and come out on top. It took for a second tragedy in her life for her to see what Aunt Pearl tried to tell her.

Aunt Pearl, Maya, and Michelle were in the kitchen, putting finishing touches on dinner. They prepared deep fried turkey, country style ribs, fresh collard greens, macaroni and cheese, cornbread, and apple pie. Loreal bounced Samiya on her lap, when there was a knock on the door. Loreal placed Samiya in her playpen and answered the door.

Loreal opened the door and there stood King. She greeted him with open arms.

"Oh, my God! We didn't expect you home yet," Loreal said.

"Are you going to let me in?" King said.

Loreal let go of King and he walked in, looking around as if it was his first time there. "Guess, who's here?" Loreal yelled out. Everyone rushed out of the kitchen.

"I'm home!" King shouted.

Maya rushed into his arms. "Baby, you're home!"

"Thank you, Jesus!" Aunt Pearl said, clapping her hands as she cried.

"They dropped the other charges. I'm home, baby. It's over," he said. He squeezed her tightly in his arms. He'd missed her so much that he vowed to never do anything to put that much time and space between them ever again.

"Thank, God! I missed you so much," Maya said.

"Where's my baby girl?" he asked. Loreal pointed to the playpen.

King reached in and picked up his baby girl. For the first time, he held her without a heavy heart. There were no more chains holding him. He looked into Samiya's eyes.

"I'm so sorry for leaving you. I promise I will never leave you again," he said. Samiya smiled and reached for his face. King kissed her.

"I promise, I will never leave you again," he told her.

The room was full of emotions. They'd missed him dearly, especially Maya. Those three months took a toll on her. Aunt Pearl spent more days with Maya than she did at her own apartment. Michelle and Loreal also spent more time with her and Samiya.

"Hey, jailbird!" Starr said. She entered the living room. She was in the back, lying down after taking a pain pill. Her shoulder still gave her problems.

"Hey, sis," he said, bouncing Samiya in his arms.

"Hey, bro," she said, punching him in the arm.

"I didn't get a chance to say it before, but thank you," King said.

"It didn't quite go as planned, but you're welcome," Starr said.

"But if you would've told me what you were planning—" King started.

"The two of you are always at it. Come on and eat," Aunt Pearl said, interrupting the impending argument.

King walked over to Aunt Pearl and gave her a tight hug, lifting her off her feet.

"Oh, my. Put me down!" she said, tapping him on his shoulder. "I've been praying for you."

"Thank you for everything you ever did for me and Happy Birthday," he said.

"This is the best birthday gift I could've asked for," Aunt Pearl said.

"Let's eat. I'm starving," King said.

That night before he went to bed, King cleaned out the basement, disposing of everything that reminded him of his past. Tone was dead. Although, that didn't bring back his mother, he felt that justice was finally served. No longer was he that angry, bloodthirsty man. The chains of grief and vengeance no longer bound him. His future was no longer tied to his past. He was a husband and father; it was the time for him to live his life and embrace happiness with no guilt. He could finally be in a room where the walls no longer cried.

FOR MORE INFORMATION VISIT THE
NATIONAL INSTITUTE ON DEAFNESS AND
OTHER COMMUNICATION DISORDERS AT
WWW.NIDCD.NIH.GOV

Amarquis Publications
Presents

KARMA'S KISS
2

SNOOK

Coming soon from Amarquis Publications

CPSIA information can be obtained at www.ICGtesting.com
Printed in the USA
BVOW08s1607200316

441044BV00001B/20/P